Doris Fein:
Dead Heat at
Long Beach

T. Ernesto Bethancourt

Holiday House/New York

Library of Congress Cataloging in Publication Data

Bethancourt, T. Ernesto.
  Doris Fein, dead heat at Long Beach.

  SUMMARY: Doris Fein and her new friend, who is a
contender for the world's race car driving championship, employ their wits and driving skills against a
group of ruthless revolutionaries.
  [1. Mystery and detective stories] I. Title.
PZ7.B46627Dom 1983   [Fic]   82-48754
ISBN 0-8234-0485-4

For SIR VICKTOR, THE GOOD

Contents

Doris Fein:
Dead Heat at Long Beach

1/ The Concrete Gumdrop

COMING OUT OF the last turn, I put my foot to the floor. I was rewarded by a rush of power that pushed me back in the driver's seat. I checked the speedometer. One hundred and sixty-five miles per hour! Yet, the car responded as surely and quickly as if I had been tooling down the San Diego Freeway at fifty-five, the legal limit. What a feeling! The only thing one can compare to high-speed driving in a fine-tuned sports car is flying.

My instructor waved me to the pit area, and I waved back as I sped down the straightaway at a conservative one hundred and ten miles per hour. Not that I couldn't have stopped. The oversized brakes on the car could have brought a tractor trailer to a stop. It was the exhilaration that drove me to go another lap on the Lakeside Speedway track.

No, I'm not a professional race driver, though there have been a few women who have chosen the career.

In fact, I'm not a professional anything, except a student at the University of California at Irvine. You may well ask what is an eighteen-year-old nice, middle-class Jewish girl doing whipping around a racetrack at over a hundred miles an hour? In a car that cost over fifty thousand dollars, at that?

The answer is complicated, but what that's interesting in life isn't? It all began when I suddenly found myself the owner of a concrete-filled sports car. I loved that car, too. I'd worked very hard to get it. For my last two years in Santa Amelia High School, in my Southern California hometown, I worked as receptionist for my dad, Dr. Michael Fein. He's an opthalmologist. My name is Doris Fein, and on occasion, I'm a spy.

That's right, a cloak-and-dagger type. Actually, all I did was act as a courier for the Information Gathering Organization, or the IGO, as we insiders call it. On another occasion, I was a decoy in a terrorist plot. After two missions for the IGO, I swore off spy biz. Too scary, too real.

Coming around on the return lap, I eased off on the gas and with light braking coasted into the pit area. Jimmy Ogilvie, my instructor, opened the door on the driver's side as I unbelted and took off my helmet.

"You did real good that time, Ms. Fein," he said. "But you're still not trusting the car going into the turns and coming out. That's where you win the races, you know."

"I'm not going to race, Jimmy," I replied. "I just want

to be able to drive safely at high speeds when the occasion comes up."

And as Lily Tomlin would say, that's the truth. I was a bit embarrassed to be the owner of a high-performance car and not know how to use it properly. I went to the water fountain and had a few sips. The water was cold, but didn't mask the fact that, like most water in Southern California, it tasted more like someone's chemistry set than *aqua pura*. Oh, our regular water supply is pure and quite safe to drink. Just unappetizing.

Jimmy Ogilvie busied himself removing the protective vinyl nose guard and other modifications he'd made on the car for high-speed running. The beauty of the red car was that once I had run it at ridiculous speeds on the raceway, I could drive it home, over the freeways.

I looked at the Red Menace. I had to admit it was sheer elegance, and outrageously extravagant. I'd only owned it for a few weeks, and was shamelessly in love with it. I must be a fickle creature. For two years, I had adored the Flying Gumdrop.

The Gumdrop was a TR-7, painted a bright candy green. Wedge-shaped, it looked like it was going a hundred miles an hour, even standing still. The Gumdrop had seen me through some wonderful, and some frightening, times. In a way, losing that car was symbolic of all the changes that have happened in my life over the past two years. It wouldn't have been destroyed if I hadn't inherited a great deal of money.

"Ready to roll, Ms. Fein," Jimmy called. "See you next week?"

"Same time?" I asked.

"I'll be here."

I gave him a wave and pulled away from the pits and onto the access road that led toward the exit gates. In a few minutes, I was buzzing down the Orange Freeway toward Santa Amelia. After the high-speed driving I'd done, it seemed the traffic was crawling along. But checking the speedometer, I saw I was moving at the prescribed fifty-five mph.

Glancing in the rear-view mirror, I saw a Japanese sports model following at an interval that was positively dangerous. I knew that changing lanes wouldn't shake the driver off. He was trying to get close enough to find out what make of car I was driving. In just two weeks' time, I was getting used to the practice. I eased up on the gas and slowed to fifty, then forty-five miles per hour, the minimum speed for California freeways. Sure enough, the Datsun 280-Z pulled around me, and I didn't miss the admiring look its driver gave as he passed.

It's California status. It may sound shallow and materialistic, but here in Southern California, to a large extent, you *are* what you drive. The entire area is a society on wheels. And because dress is inevitably casual, what you wear is not important. Consequently the symbol of your achievements, to those who don't know you, is the automobile you own.

The exit for Santa Amelia came up, and I signaled at

the proper time. In a few minutes, I was driving up to the gates of the huge old Victorian mansion I call home these days. I flipped a switch on the dash, and the iron gates swung silently open.

As I turned into the big winding driveway that leads to the house, two dark forms skimmed across the greensward circle formed by the approach road. Two beautiful Alsatian shepherds, black as night, were standing at attention when I pulled up at the front portico, their tails awag and their tongues lolling out in doggy mirth.

Their names are Rover and Rover. The man I inherited them from, Harry Grubb, had a rather primitive sense of humor. He acquired the Alsatians as guard dogs for the big estate, and promptly dubbed them the Rover Boys: Rover and Rover. Harry Grubb was what is called eccentric. That's when someone is too rich and powerful to be called plain old-fashioned nuts.

But if Harry Grubb was crazy, he was crazy like a fox. For years, he'd been a crime reporter for the *Chicago Tribune*. Then, late in life, he'd married a very wealthy widow. She died after only a year and a half of marriage. Harry then moved to Santa Amelia, ostensibly to write his memoirs. Trouble was, the inactivity maddened him.

He bought a huge house and lovingly refurbished it. He bought a monstrous yacht and tired of it. What he really wanted to do was go back to crime reporting. But at age seventy-five, no one would hire him. His solution to the problem was typical of Harry. He bought our local newspaper, *The Register*, and installed himself as chief crime reporter. That's when I first met him.

I was instrumental in the solving of an assassination attempt on Danny Breckinridge, the rock star. Perhaps you know him better as Dr. Doom. In the course of the case, Harry and I became loving adversaries, and later shared a number of adventures. When he died accidentally a year ago, I was shocked and bereaved.

I was even more shocked to discover that, lacking any living close relatives, he'd left the bulk of his fortune to me! I inherited literally millions. Plus *The Santa Amelia Register*, a losing basketball team called the Saints, a controlling interest in the corporation that ran the Santa Amelia Municipal Arena, the Rover Boys, the big Victorian house, and, in an odd way, the man who opened the front door of the house as I stepped from the Red Menace.

A bit under six feet tall, constructed along the lines of a professional wrestler, and dressed in formal butler's garb, Alois "Bruno" Biegler greeted me in his usual fashion: dead silence.

"Hi, Bruno," I chirped. "Any calls?"

"No, Ms. Fein," he replied.

I didn't wait for further amplification, nor for chitchat. Bruno hardly ever speaks more than a few words. He can't. It's an odd mental disability Bruno has had since he was a child. Just a bit shy of autism, he is almost incapable of volunteering any information unless directly asked. Even then, you must know how to draw the knowledge you want from him with skillful questioning. I guess the best comparison is a computer.

You see, there's nothing wrong with Bruno's mental capacity. In fact, he's a master of many intricate skills. But all the data are locked up inside his head by his strange condition. He's incredibly loyal to me, but I feel it's mostly because Harry Grubb told him to be. Bruno worshipped Harry Grubb. With good cause. Harry's investigative reporting cleared Bruno of murdering his parents.

Bruno was innocent, of course. But when he was found with a bloodied knife in his parents' home, his condition couldn't let him explain that he'd merely discovered the bodies. He was convicted and spent years in a hospital for the criminally insane. Until Harry's investigating exonerated him. When he was freed, he went to work for Harry and devoted the rest of his life to him. When Harry died, Bruno stayed on with me. He gives a lot of people the willies. Not me, though. I think that as much as he can care for anyone since Harry died, Bruno is fond of me.

I entered the house, and from one of the downstairs rooms I heard the strains of Beethoven's *Für Elise*. Obviously a student playing, not Helen Grayson. Helen is a marvelous lady in her sixties who shares the big house with Bruno and me. She teaches piano to talented underprivileged kids. I finance it. Why not? I have more money than I could ever spend.

I went up to my room on the second floor. It was like stepping into another house: my Dad's and Mom's. When I'd inherited the big house, I just wasn't comfortable with all the artwork and antiques that Harry had accumulated. So I had the furniture from my old room at home moved to the big house. It suits me better.

I surveyed myself in the full-length mirror as I unzipped my silver, fire-retardant driving suit. I'm five feet four inches tall and, depending on my willpower, anywhere from five to fifteen pounds overweight. If you believe in those height-weight charts. They say I should weigh less, but frankly, I think my bones alone weigh the indicated weight for five foot four. Face it. A sylph I'm not.

But I have attractive hazel eyes and medium brown hair that has light streaks in summer. And really great teeth. My best feature, courtesy of my Uncle Saul, the dentist. I still have vivid memories of when I had a mouthful of orthodontic silver, weighed forty-five pounds too much, and had a complexion like a pizza.

I peeled off my underclothes, slipped into my favorite pink terry robe, and padded down the corridor to the master suite. I don't sleep there, even though I own the house. It's all oversized. Harry was six feet three inches tall. Every time I go into the master suite, I feel like the Incredible Shrinking Doris.

Ah, but the bathroom! That's another story. It, too, is outsized, but absolutely sybaritic in its appointments. The marble tub is so big that one only worries about two things: drowning while asleep, or submarine attacks. I poured some Lactopine Verbena into the thundering hot water from the tap and watched it form mountains of deliciously scented bubbles. The temperature adjusted, I sank into the bubbly alps of suds and luxuriated.

Only two weeks earlier, I'd consoled myself in this same tub over the loss of the Gumdrop. I'd been heart-broken. It had happened while I was having lunch with my good friend, Vick Knight.

Vick is director of community relations for Children's Hospital of Orange County, or as it's known to coun-tians, CHOC. I've known Vick for ages through my mother's volunteer work at CHOC and her member-ship in the CHOC Guild. Naturally, when Mom and I drew up a list of worthy causes to which I'd contribute annually, CHOC was high on the list.

In choosing Vick to represent them to the commu-nity, CHOC made a marvelous choice. He's a big kid himself. Not that he isn't very capable at his job. He's won awards for his work. But as he puts it, "Who said you can't have fun at what you do?"

And have fun, he does. In the process, he's also done wonderful things for the children of Orange County. He's a dynamo of a man, about my height and my old weight. He has silvery hair, a matching beard, sparkling blue eyes, and one of the quickest wits in California. He resembles an impish Santa Claus, but is only in his early fifties.

His rotund figure bespeaks his passion for good food and California wines, which he bottles himself. Vick knows every good-to-great restaurant in the state. He always meets me for lunch, and I agonize over my salads and Perrier while he eats food that makes me gain weight just watching *him* eat it.

That day, I was meeting him at a new restaurant he'd discovered. It was a French restaurant in an unlikely place, adjacent to an office building, still under construction. In fact, half the restaurant parking lot was out of service. Heavy equipment had encroached on their space. I pulled the Gumdrop around a big cement truck and found that the construction hadn't daunted the patrons of the restaurant. The lot was jammed.

I parked closer than I should have to the huge crane that was lifting iron buckets of concrete up to the higher floors of the building under construction. I hurried into the restaurant and entered a different world.

All the noise of the building site was shut out, and I found myself in a charming eating place that wouldn't have been unusual on the Right Bank, in Paris.

An impeccably turned out maître d' guided me to Vick's table. He was going over some facts and figures when I got there. He got to his feet, and I obediently accepted a hug and a kiss on the cheek.

"Hi, dearie," he said cheerfully. "How's the poor little rich girl today?"

"Not funny," I replied. "My money has jerked me around more than it's benefited me. I never know if people are sharing my company because of me or it."

"That's the beautiful part of our relationship, my little chickadee," he drawled in an excellent W. C. Fields impression. "You *know* I'm after your money. Or at least the kids of Orange County are."

"I was wonderin' why you never c'mup and see me," I said in my best Mae West tones.

It's a running gag with Vick and me, the Fields-West routines. Vick is president of the W. C. Fields Fan Club of North America or, as it's properly known, The Bank Dicks. In fact, a few years back, when the U.S. government issued a Fields commemorative postage stamp, it was Vick's doing. He'd introduced the idea and lobbied it through passage.

"Enough of this badinage, m'dear," he said. "Let's do something important. Like order lunch. Unless you want to run away with me to Baja California for a lust-filled weekend."

"Okay with me, if your wife agrees," I quipped.

"Darnit!" he said. "I knew you'd think of that. But I want to do something in return for your contributions to CHOC."

"You don't have to work it out in trade," I came back. "Besides, at your rates, I can't afford you."

Our waitress arrived, and Vick ordered for us both in excellent French. When lunch arrived, he'd ordered a seafood crepe for me, with just a touch of Sauce Mornay. The crepe was delicious, but I knew I'd pay for the sauce with at least two hours of workouts.

"You are absolutely corrupting me, sir," I told him.

"If I can't getcha one way, I'll try another," he said, digging into a *boeuf en brochette* on rice that made Petunia growl.

Petunia is my alter ego. Doris Fein is a nice, sensible young woman who watches her diet, takes regular ex-

ercise, and fights valiantly not to resemble a Goodyear
Blimp. Petunia Fein is capable of knocking off a half-
gallon of Baskin-Robbins Rocky Road à la mode at one
sitting. That's with another half-gallon of Jamocha Al-
mond Fudge on top of it. With nuts. And cherries.
Maybe a touch of whipped cream . . . Oink!

I watched him demolish the beef, washing it down
with a fine California Cabernet Sauvignon as I drank
Perrier with lime. While he had a brandy and coffee
and I an iced tea with Sweet 'n' Low, he filled me in on
current plans for CHOC. It was to include a special
showing of Ringling Brothers Circus for the CHOC
kids.

"You'll attend, naturally?" I asked.

"Attend?" he said. "I want to be *in* it!"

"I sometimes think you set these things up for your
own personal pleasure, Vick."

"Me?" he said, his eyes rolling upward in mock inno-
cence.

"Yes, you. I think you're the biggest kid of all."

"Guilty," he admitted. "But who said you can't do
good for others and still have fun doing it?"

"I don't know. Maybe it was John Calvin."

"Forget him. He doesn't live in the neighborhood,
anyway." He took another sip of wine. "Now, to sordid
details. About your annual check."

"Already cut and signed," I said. "You'll get it from
my lawyer, Brian Donnelly, any day now."

"Are you trying to tell me that my check is in the
mail?" he asked, his eyes twinkling.

"Just so."

"Then why meet me here?"

"To tell the truth, I enjoy your company, Vick. You make me laugh."

"Funny. That's what my wife said the night we were married."

We lingered over lunch, then left together. Vick had to show me his new car, a little import with enough gadgets on it to please any Southern Californian. I was *soo* lucky he did, too. I had just got my hug and kiss good-bye and was walking back to the Gumdrop when it happened.

High above the parking lot, the crane was swinging a huge iron bucket of concrete onto the upper floor of the building. I don't know exactly what happened with the crane, or its controls. But suddenly, the bucket broke loose on one side and who-knows-how-many thousand pounds of wet cement came thundering down. Right on top of my beautiful little TR-7!

2/ The Red Menace

VICK WAS AT my side in an instant. "Are you all right, Doris?" he asked.

I couldn't answer. I was in total shock. If I hadn't gone to look at Vick's new car, I would have been under that gloppy mass of concrete. And very, verry dead! I couldn't help it, I began to shake all over.

Vick guided me back into the restaurant and in a short time handed me a glass. Abstractedly, I took a sip. I nearly choked. It was cognac.

"Hey, don't spill that stuff," Vick said. "It's seventy-five years old!" He took the glass and put a hand to my cheek. "You look poor, dearie," he said.

"Ever the flatterer, eh?" I gasped through cognac fumes. I don't drink. Maybe a glass of white wine with a meal, or champagne on special occasions. The cognac hit my stomach, and a warmth spread from there all over my body.

16

Vick laughed louder and longer than he should have at my reply. "Now I know you're all right," he said.

We sat there for about fifteen minutes until I got control; then Vick took me outside again. I surveyed the mess that had been my car. I couldn't bear to see it that way. Vick took me to his car, and we left the lot. There was a crowd of passersby and construction workers gathered around the cement Gumdrop.

"Shouldn't I stay there?" I asked as we drove away from the parking lot. "Won't someone want to take a statement, or something?"

"You're in no shape," Vick said, shifting gears. "And besides, no one's going to tow your car away. They'd have to dig it out first."

"I guess you're right. But oh, Vick. It was awful!"

"Take it easy, Doris," he advised. "I'll get you home, and then you can get busy."

"At what?"

"Looking at new car ads, of course," he replied. "The best medicine for a broken heart is a new car. If you don't drink, that is," he added. He laughed. "I think you've got a swell lawsuit against the construction company. I'll be your witness, for a slight fee."

"What kind of fee? I already gave at my lawyer's office."

"I had something else in mind. An invitation to dinner at your house. Bruno's Beef Wellington would be nice."

"Sold," I said. "That'll be you, Carolyn, and your girls?"

"Just me and Carolyn," he said. "My girls have their own social set. I have the suspicion they don't think I'm dignified enough."

"They're quite right, of course," I replied.

As Bruno served the chocolate mousse, I felt my reserve weakening. All through dinner with Helen Grayson, Vick Knight, and his wife Carolyn, I had doggedly stayed with my Caesar salad and Perrier, while I had to watch the others fall to on Bruno's Beef Wellington.

Despite the incredible wine cellar that came with the big old house, Vick had brought a special California Cabernet Sauvignon to have with dinner. I'd had a small sip. It would have been rude not to. Superb. We chatted about current events and the low state of the arts but laughed at Vick's stories more than anything else. He's very much in demand as an after-dinner speaker, and he's no slouch *during* dinner, either. Before we knew it, it was close to ten o'clock.

"That about does it for me," Vick said, glancing at his watch. "Six o'clock in the morning comes early, and I have a long drive ahead of me."

"Who told you to move way out to Canyon Lake?" I asked. Vick lives about as far away from the center of Orange County as one can get.

"A real estate agent," he responded. "I took one look at the prices, and after my blood pressure came back to normal, I discovered Canyon Lake. I'm no millionaire, like some people I know."

"Don't keep reminding me," I said. "The money is a burden."

"Then unburden yourself on us," Carolyn urged. "We have strong shoulders."

"True," Vick said. "Carolyn can carry off at least a million. I'm not big, but I can make two trips."

"It's all in trust, anyway," I said. "Any expenditures I make have to be cleared through Brian Donnelly." I smiled. "He has a fine grip on the dollar."

"I don't trust the man," Vick said in his Fields impression, "Any Irishman who doesn't drink is suspect, in my mind."

"Anyone at all who doesn't drink is suspect," Carolyn said. "Vick is very egalitarian that way."

"Regardless of race, religion, or national origin," Vick added.

"Speaking of such things, I have to see Brian tomorrow about what happened to my car," I said. "I inherited two others, but I can't see myself driving to school in a Mercedes-Benz 600 sedan."

"What's the other car?" Vick asked.

"That one makes me even more uncomfortable," I replied. "It's a museum piece. A 1936 model-316 Cord Phaeton."

Vick whistled in appreciation. "A beautiful machine," he said. "And worth a fortune. I heard of one in mint condition going for over a quarter of a million bucks."

"How much?" I squeaked.

"Twenty-five, with four zeros behind it," Vick affirmed. "Don't you know what your own car is worth?"

"I inherited it from Harry Grubb," I said. "I knew it was valuable, but that's outrageous. I can't even work the gearshift properly. They have this thingie on the steering column. You shift gears with your little finger."

"It's a gear preselector," Vick said.

"You seem to be filled with automotive lore," I said. "I know you're a reptile expert. Is this car thing something new?"

"You could say so," he replied. "I recently met a fascinating fellow. Name of Cavalieri."

"Sounds Italian."

"Give that lady a cigar for being bright," he said. "Anyway, Albert sells used cars."

"Hardly a rarity in Orange County," I said. "I sometimes think that all of Costa Mesa is one big car lot."

"Perhaps calling Albert a used-car dealer is misleading," Vick said. "The used cars he sells are Rolls-Royces, Ferraris, and Lamborghinis. He sells new cars, too." Vick smiled. "I could live for a year on what he sells in a week. And I'd like to, at that."

"And you think I ought to buy a Rolls?" I asked. "I'm no . . ." I suddenly stopped myself. I was about to say I was no millionaire, either. But it wasn't true. I am a millionaire. Thirty million, in fact. I just can't conceive of such amounts. Not when you consider that up until a year ago, I was living on an allowance from my dad and living at home.

"You were saying," said Carolyn, "that you're not what?"

"That I'm not about to go tootling around UCI in a Rolls," I said, recovering neatly. "Even if I could afford it. I loved my little TR-7. A two-seater suits me perfectly."

"Albert has those, too," Vick said. "A very special kind of car. He designed it himself."

"Pretty ambitious for a car seller," I commented.

"Not when you consider that he's an automotive engineer and a graduate of Northrup University. Why don't you meet me at his showroom tomorrow? Say, about lunchtime? I know this marvelous Italian restaurant in Corona Del Mar. La Strada."

"I'll pass on lunch," I said. "Just hanging out with you makes me gain weight. I've been doing so well on my diet, and every time I see you for lunch, you add to the temptation."

"And like Oscar Wilde, that's the only thing you can't resist?"

"You got it, round fella," I said.

We got up from the table and walked toward the door. Bruno materialized with Carolyn's coat and Vick's cowboy hat. I walked them to their car. The Rovers patrol after dark, and Bruno, Helen, and I are the only ones who can call them off. As they were about to drive off, Vick leaned out the window and said, "Don't forget. It's Tempo Imports. Directly opposite the Cortez Bay Yacht Club. You know where that is?"

"You forget that I'm a member of the club and have

a monstrous yacht there," I said. It's true. Harry's float-
ing palace, *The Parvenu*, is tied up at the Cortez.

"Great!" Vick said. "See you tomorrow." He drove off
and honked when he reached the gate at the end of the
drive. Bruno pushed the release, and I heard the buzz
of Vick's little car engine as they left.

Even though it was late, I went to Harry's office and,
with Bruno's help, went over all crime stories in *The
Register* for the day, entering them into my computer
crime files.

Harry started recording all unsolved crimes or ques-
tionable cases years ago. He has virtually every crime
of passion or profit entered on computer disks. They're
all cross-indexed as to date, age, and sex of offender,
motive, geographical locations . . . you name it. I discovered the files behind a sliding panel in Harry's office a
short time ago. Harry had Bruno trained to operate the
machine. Bruno is a computer whiz. We worked together for an hour, then I went off to bed, to a deep,
dreamless sleep. . . .

"It's gorgeous!" I exclaimed. "I have never in my life
seen . . ."

"Naturally," Vick said. "There's never been one of
these before."

I walked around the red car that was the center at-
traction of the Tempo Imports showroom. Vick had
been right. Tempo is hardly a used-car lot. The showroom had crystal chandeliers! Over the last half-hour, I
had looked at some of the most exotic automobiles in

the world. Vick had acted as my guide, though there were salespeople available. They didn't keep hanging about us, though. I commented on that to Vick. Usually, when you walk into a place in Southern California that sells cars, you immediately acquire an ugly growth. It's called a car salesman.

"Of course they don't bother you," Vick explained. "Unless you ask for help. Face it, I don't care what kind of hot-shot salesperson you are, you *can't* sell someone a fifty-thousand-dollar car. No one could. The customer buys it; it's not sold."

"Makes sense," I admitted. "And it is nice not to be bothered while you're looking. But oh, Vick! This car! What kind is it?"

"Funny you should ask," he said. "That's the Cavalieri 400 GT Spyder. Zero to sixty miles per hour in four seconds flat. Top speed, depending on which engine you choose, is anywhere from one-forty to two hundred seventy-five miles per hour."

"You mean *one* hundred seventy-five miles per hour, don't you?" I asked.

"I'm a man who says what he means," he drawled in W. C. Fields fashion. "That's *two* hundred seventy-five. Yet the car is legal to drive on the streets and freeways. You can't even say that about the Ferrari Boxer in stock condition. And the Ferrari can't even crack the two-hundred-mile-an-hour mark."

"But Vick, this is all silly. The legal speed limit any-where in the U.S.A. is fifty-five. What's the point of having such a hairy car?"

He didn't answer. He simply opened the door on the driver's side and waved me inside. I fell in love on the spot. The interior was of the finest leather. There's no mistaking that scent. The dash and panels were matched grain rosewood. The seats were infinitely adjustable and power-driven, as were the windows and steering. The steering wheel was also adjustable, and I fiddled until it came into exactly the right position.

The rosewood-encircled dash contained enough instrumentation to surpass the control panel of my Piper Apache. And just for fun, there was an AM/FM radio, with front and rear speakers. The car was simply the most luxurious and powerful machine I'd ever seen or heard of.

"I love it!" I said to Vick. "I covet this car. I haven't felt this way about an inanimate object in my life."

"Shhh!" Vick said. "Albert may be here, somewhere. Never say inanimate. I have a suspicion that Albert feels his cars have souls."

I climbed out of the posh embrace of the driver's seat, regretfully. I sighed deeply. "Okay, Vick. How much is it?"

"I'm no salesman," he said. "But there's a list of prices in the brochures, over there." He walked over to a desk and came back with an illustrated flier. "Let's see . . ." he said. "If you want one equipped just like the one you were sitting in . . . um . . ."

"Don't keep me hanging," I said. "How much?"

"A mere pittance," he said with a grin. "Only fifty thousand dollars."

I nearly fainted dead away. "That's a fortune!" I gasped.

"Depends on how you look at it," Vick said casually. "It's considerably less than a Rolls-Royce Corniche convert. Or a number of other cars here. In fact, the brochure says that the fifty grand is an introductory price. It's expected that future Cavalieris will cost closer to one hundred and fifty thou."

"You certainly have a flair for throwing my money around," I said.

"Flair? I have a gift for it. Vicarious thrills, m'dear. When I first saw the Cavalieri, I wanted one. Then I slunk out to my Mazda GLC Sport and putted home. I'll never own one. But I said to myself: 'Self, if someone you know has one, maybe she'll let you drive it . . . just once.'"

"Dream on, my friend. I can't afford it, either."

"Doris, you have millions," he replied.

"All in trust, and accountable to Brian Donnelly. I can just see me calling him and saying I want a new car . . . and by the way, I can get a swell bargain for fifty thousand dollars. He'd have apoplexy!"

"It couldn't hoit to call," Vick said.

"You really want a free ride in one, don't you?"

"Guilty, as usual. But there's more to it than a heavy price tag, Doris. This car is going to appreciate in value, not decrease, after you buy it."

"I haven't bought it."

"All right, after you buy it, *if* you buy it. For instance, that Cord in your garage. Brand-new, it sold for less than a tenth of its current value. There are many people who invest in high-value cars, just like some people buy art objects. This car could make money for you."

"Tell you what, you silver-tongued devil," I told him. "*You* talk to Brian Donnelly. I'll call him. Do they have a conference phone here?"

"In the office. I'll see if Albert's here." He went off to the back of the showroom and returned in a few seconds. "Okay, we can use the one in that office over there," he said, indicating an ornate door. In a minute, Brian Donnelly was on the phone with both of us.

I told him about the beautiful car. Vick gave him all the specifications on the car and its background. Then Donnelly asked the fatal question: how much?

"Fifty thousand dollars," I told him, my voice shaking. A dead silence ensued.

"One moment," came his dry-as-dust voice over the conference phone. "I have to make some calculations."

"I told you he'd have a hernia," I whispered to Vick.

"You said apoplexy," Vick shot back. "A hernia is at the other end."

"Ms. Fein?" came Donnelly's voice over the speaker.

"Still here," I answered. "What's the good news?"

"If Mr. Knight's estimate of appreciation is correct, I have no objection to your having this car. That is, if proper care is taken to preserve the investment."

"What?" I yelped in astonishment. "Fifty thousand? Can I really afford that much for a car, Mr. Donnelly?"

In a voice that sounded like dead leaves being swept from a concrete patio, he said: "Ms. Fein, your investment portfolio earns you about twelve thousand dollars a day. Yes, you can afford it. You can place your order, and refer the business details to my office." With no further comment, he broke the connection, and the dial tone hum came over the conference speaker. Vick and I sat in silence, looking at each other.

"Well, I'll be . . ." I began.

"Naughty, naughty," he said, waggling a finger. "And if anyone'll be . . . It'll probably be me. I have much more practice at sin than you do." He stood up. "Now, shall we rustle up a salesperson and buy a car? I can't wait to drive it!"

"Greedy, greedy," I said as we went back to the showroom.

Two days later, with Vick in attendance, my new car arrived. It was blood-red in color. That's the one option you don't have with the Cavalieri car. You can have any color you desire—so long as it's red.

But there was a consolation prize, of course. When I was given the key to my new 400 GT. The key to this car comes in a little velvet jewelry box. It should. It's made by a jewelry store in Los Angeles, and it's fourteen-karat gold!

3/ George T. Case Again

I BEGAN TO look forward to my weekly lessons at the raceway. Jimmy Ogilvie was a fine teacher and had been a race driver himself until he lost an argument with a retaining wall at over 150 miles per hour. The accident had left him with a leg full of metal pins and a permanent limp. To combat the inactivity, Jim had opened a high-speed driving school at the track.

The lessons weren't cheap. Not because of Jim's charges, which were modest, but to get the time on the raceway in which to learn was expensive. I had exactly ninety minutes, once a week. There were always people waiting for their time on the circuit, so being at the track on time was important. The fees went on whether one was there or not.

I was making my last lap and heading toward the pits. Suddenly, with an unbelievable roar, a car sped by me on the outside. I had thought I was alone on the big oval, and the apparition of the full formula car that blew by me momentarily caused me to lose control of the Red Menace. I fishtailed a few times, and finally managed to correct. I eased the red car into the pits. Jim came over immediately.

"What's going on?" I demanded even before Jim got to the car. "I thought I had the track to myself."

"So did I," Jim said. "Whoever that is in that formula car is dangerous. And irresponsible, too."

"I'm going to find out who that hot dog is," I said as I unbelted and took off my helmet. I watched the formula car as it roared around the track. "Does the car look familiar to you, Jim?"

"Sure," he said. "It's a McClaren. But all formula cars look alike. Only made by a handful of firms. If you want to wait at the pits until that driver is done, I'll go with you. I got a few words to say to that bird. And they ain't *happy* and *birthday.*"

We waited just outside the line at the pit area for the car that had nearly caused me grief. Finally, the brutish-looking machine pulled into the service area. The driver wore the full helmet and fire-retardant suit that are standard with race drivers of formula cars. I had no idea what he looked like until he was assisted from the cocoon of the race car and shed his helmet.

He was a bit under six feet tall, with dark, curly hair. His features were sharp, with a longish, high-bridged nose flanked by dark, piercing eyes. He was slim but athletically built. I strode angrily up to him.

"I don't know who you are," I began heatedly, "but

you're some kind of fool, or a madman! You blew me right off the track. I had to fight to control my car. My track time wasn't up yet. I intend to report you to the track officials for endangering the lives of others. I have seen carelessness, but this is—"

I broke off. The man was standing there, nodding his head and smiling. He had beautiful teeth and a warm smile. I was also of the opinion that somewhere, there was a hole in that head of dark, curly hair.

"Do you think this all a joke?" I demanded.

"Hardly, my dear lady," he said with a touch of a Latin accent.

"I'm not *your* dear anything," I snapped. "And I'm about to say something no lady would."

"My humblest apologies," he said, that condescending grin never leaving his face. "I thought I'd come onto the track at exactly my appointed time. It was an error."

"Once you saw me, you could have slowed down until I got to the pits."

"Dear lady," he drawled, "I *did* slow down. My car is an extremely powerful one. I deeply regret the inconvenience I have caused you."

"Inconvenience?" I snorted. "I could have been killed!"

He shrugged and spread his hands apart. "Everyone dies, dear lady. But rarely on a racetrack. I'm sure you are in much more danger on your freeways, here in California. I assumed you were a professional driver like myself, and wouldn't be frightened by a car passing you."

"I wasn't frightened," I said heatedly. "I was startled. I thought I was alone on the track."

"There you are," he said with an oleaginous smile. "You should realize that an attractive woman is never alone. So long as there are gentlemen with taste and good eyesight. Allow me to make this up to you. May I take you to dinner?"

"You're impossible!" I sputtered.

"True, but also contrite," he answered. "Will you join me for dinner? I know the best of places in Los Angeles." He pronounced the name of the city as a Spanish-speaking person would: *Lohs AHN-hay-lace.*

"So do I," I retorted, "and I don't dine with strangers. Especially idiots who imperil lives!"

"A thousand pardons," he said. "We have not been introduced. I am Roderigo Alfonso Alcala, *a sus órdenes:* at your service."

"Good-bye, Mr. Alcala," I said, and began walking away.

"Wait, please wait," he entreated. "How can I apologize properly? I don't even know your name!"

"Doris Fein," I said over my shoulder. "Ms. Doris Fein."

I walked quickly back to my car. Alcala got there before Jimmy could open the door. I don't care to have car doors opened for me. There's nothing wrong with me physically. In fact, ever since I visited a *verry* exclusive health spa, I'm in better condition than I've ever been. So when Alcala swung the door open, I didn't get inside. I stood glaring at him, standing there with a professionally charming smile on his face.

I've seen the type before. All Latin macho, convinced that any woman in her right mind would fall down and kiss his feet, just to be noticed by His Wonderfulness. I was about to comment when he began looking over my car. Suddenly, all his Latin-lover demeanor was gone. He became a small boy, looking over a brand-new set of electric trains.

"I have never seen such a car," he said, peering inside the interior. "Beautifully executed GT car. What's the power plant?"

"Four hundred cubic inches," I said. "It's a GM engine with turbo/water injection."

He whistled softly. "Almost six liters," he said. "It has to put out over four hundred horsepower."

"Five hundred," I corrected, brushing past him and getting behind the wheel. I tossed my helmet onto the passenger seat. He was still blocking the door on the driver's side. "Do you mind?" I asked pointedly. He stepped back and I closed the door. I fired up the Red Menace's hairy power plant. I must admit that I gave it a bit more loud pedal than necessary. He took another step backward and I pulled away. I saw him in my rear-view mirror talking animatedly to Jimmy. In a few minutes, I was on my way home.

When I got back to Santa Amelia and my big house, Bruno had a message for me. From Alcala. Another apology, with his phone number. I glanced casually at the exchange. It was an Orange County number. I would have guessed Newport Beach. I crumpled up the message and tossed it at the basket near the door. I missed. Bruno picked it up before I could get to it. He looked askance at me.

"No return message, Bruno," I said as I went upstairs to wash the grime of the road off. He sure didn't waste any time, I thought as I walked up the stairs. He must have got my number from Jimmy Ogilvie. In a few minutes, I was soaking in my marble bath, with any thought of the arrogant Señor Alcala far from my mind.

I spent most of the late afternoon working on a paper for my anthropology class, and by the time Petunia began grumbling about dinner, my mind was awhirl with endogomy, bride stealing, folkways, and mores. I'd just put aside my texts when the intercom buzzed at my bedside.

"Yes, Bruno?" I said.

"Dinner at seven for three," he said. "Menu is prepared."

"For three?" I asked. "Who are we expecting?"

"The vet," he said. "Dr. Cane."

"Omigosh, I forgot all about it!" I cried. Dr. Cane had been taking care of the Rovers and my Siamese cats since my old veterinarian retired. I feel funny calling him "doctor," though. He's very young. When he first came to my house, it was to treat one of the Rovers. A piano student of Helen Grayson's had arrived on a motorcycle and gotten entangled with one of my Alsatians.

Dr. Cane had not only treated Rover wonderfully, but even boarded him. I'd been involved in a light plane crash, and Cane knew I couldn't have coped with an injured animal. I was in the hospital myself.

I'd been very taken with the way Cane handled animals. Rover absolutely fawned on him. This, from a guard dog, is extraordinary. Guard dogs are trained to regard all strangers as potential hors d'oeuvres.

There was more to this young vet. When Rover had been hit, he knew without my telling him that the machine which did the damage was a motorcycle. I knew I hadn't told him. And certainly Bruno hadn't. Not to a stranger. To strangers, Bruno is positively laconic, verging on sphinxlike.

It had been puzzling me, how Cane knew. Once before, I'd invited him to dinner, just to find out, but he'd avoided the subject. Then, with my cement-filled car and my purchase of the Red Menace, the new dinner date had slipped from my mind. I glanced at my watch. He'd be here shortly.

"What's the menu?" I asked Bruno.

"Roast orange stuffed duck, with Grand Marnier sauce. Wild rice and asparagus hollandaise," Bruno said. "Your chef's salad, as usual."

"Wine?"

"I have a Page Mill Chardonnay, 1980."

"Wonderful," I said. "I may have a teensy glass myself."

I hung up the phone. It wasn't rude to do. Bruno never says good-bye; he just hangs up after his message is delivered. In a way, it bothers me. I know he doesn't mean any offense. But I hate to hear that click. So I have adopted the practice of hanging up first.

I went to my closet. No sense in dressing up, I thought. This isn't any formal dinner. I selected a nice pair of designer jeans and a matching cashmere pullover. I was making a few passes at my hair with a brush when the intercom buzzed again.

"Forget something, Bruno?" I said into the phone.

"No, Ms. Fein. You have callers. Should I let them in?"

"Who are they, Bruno?"

"I only have one name. George T. Case. He says he knows you."

"He does indeed, Bruno. Buzz them past the gate. I'll see them in Harry's study. And if Dr. Cane gets here before Case leaves, put him in the drawing room."

"Yes, Ms. Fein.". . . *Click!* Darnit! Bruno had done it to me again. I hurried through brushing my hair and went to Harry's study. I must stop calling it that—it's mine now. I got there just as Bruno was leaving the room. He held open the door and I entered.

A thin, short man I didn't recognize was seated in one of the leather wing chairs that faces my desk. Standing with his back to me and examining a Remington bronze was a middle-sized, middle-aged, middling bald man. Unmistakably George T. Case: director of the IGO.

"Yes, it's real, Mr. Case," I said without preamble. "I have several others as well. I didn't know you were an art fancier."

Case turned, and although I know it cost him some effort, he arranged his features into what some might call a smile.

"Doris," he said jovially, "how very good to see you again!"

"I'm surprised you could face me again," I replied, "considering that the last time I worked for you, I was nearly killed. And if it comes right down to it, *every* time we've met, I've ended up in deep trouble of some sort."

"Really unforeseen, both times," he said in a conciliatory tone.

I sniffed and took his outstretched hand without much enthusiasm. I went around the desk and sat in its big swivel chair. The unidentified man blinked a bit at my display of near-rudeness. I assume he was shocked by my attitude toward his boss. After all, Case is the director of one of the most powerful intelligence agencies in the world.

The silent young man couldn't know why I felt this way, but I still get the chills remembering how I was almost murdered in the London underground, nearly a year ago. None of it would have happened if Case had been honest with me about the nature of my assignment.

"Now, what's this all about?" I asked of Case. "I know it's no social call. And to bring you all the way from Maryland, it must be important. I'm flattered, in a backhanded way."

"You flatter *yourself*," Case said, easing into the

other leather wing chair. "I was out here, anyway."

"Well, whatever it is, Mr. Case," I said, "you'll forgive my lack of enthusiasm. I'm lucky to be alive after that last assignment. The one you told me was absolutely safe. I don't work for the IGO anymore. And I doubt anything you have to say would change my mind."

Case grinned slyly. "A closed mind is a symptom of an insecure person," Case said. "You mean to tell me that you aren't even the least bit curious about what brings me to California?"

There he had me. I must confess that I'm an incurable snoop. I always have been. On many occasions, my curiosity has got me into a peck of trouble. In fact, my bump of inquisitiveness has nearly been my undoing in the past. But as a chronic eater can only arrest her condition, not cure it, so it goes with my nosiness. I didn't want to give George Case the satisfaction, so I masked my curiosity with a brisk manner. I glanced at my Omega and said, "I'm expecting a dinner guest in about twenty minutes. If you can state your business in that short a time, fine. Never let it be said I turned something down without knowing what it was."

Case turned to the slim man at his right. "Open it up, Ginsberg," he said. The slim man reached down and picked up an attaché case that leaned against the side of his chair. He set it on his lap and opened it. The case contained a compact recording machine, which he set on the desk in front of me. He produced a set of papers, which he slid across the desk to me.

I glanced at the papers. I'd seen them before. Security precautions. The forms were to be signed before I could even hear about Case's mission to Southern California.

"I'm already cleared for whatever's necessary, am I not?" I asked of Case.

"As of last year, you were," Case said easily, "but you are attending college nearby. Who knows who you've been hanging out with?"

"The University of California at Irvine is hardly a hotbed of radical types," I countered. "The average students I know there are far more concerned with their grades and their love lives than politics."

"Humor me," Case said, nodding at the forms. "Unless, of course, you don't want to know what it's all about . . ."

"All right, all right," I said, and signed the forms with my desk set pen, a Tiffany's special. I slid the papers back to the man Case called Ginsberg, who checked them and put them back into his attaché case. To Ginsberg, I said, "Tell me, what's a nice Jewish boy doing working for this master of deception?" He didn't answer. He just switched on the recorder and intoned, "April twelfth. Santa Amelia California. Interview Doris Fein, her home. Present: Director G. T. Case, Agent Ginsberg, and subject. Overt recording . . ." Ginsberg glanced over at Case and nodded.

"*Now* can you tell me what this is all about?" I inquired heavily. "My dinner guest will be here any minute."

"First," Case said, "what's your connection with Roderigo Alcala?"

"Who?" I asked. "I never heard of him."

"Oh, come now, Ms. Fein," Case said. "You were seen in his company at Lakeside Raceway this afternoon. Ginsberg spotted you. There was too much background noise to monitor your conversation with him, but you seemed fairly chatty. What's your connection?"

"Oh, him!" I said. I'd nearly forgotten all about that Latin-lover type, with all that had been going on. "I have no connection whatever with him. He nearly got me killed with his crazy driving today. I told him off. That's not being chatty."

"And you have no idea who he is?" Case asked.

"Nope, and no desire to find out. I don't care for macho types. Did you know that after running me off the track, he wanted to take me to dinner?"

"I hope you accepted," Case said.

"Hardly. I cut him off at the knees and drove home. He had phoned before I got here. I didn't return the call."

"Then it can still be salvaged," Case said.

"What can?" I asked. "It seems to me that I'm answering all the questions here. I don't know any more about your newest plot than I did before I signed the forms. What is it you want of me?"

"Well, in the interest of your government," Case said, "and in the interest of international amity and security . . . we'd like you to have dinner with him. And, um, romance him a bit."

4 / The Rundown on Snotty Roddy

"IF YOU'RE SAYING what I think you're saying, you're talking to the wrong woman," I replied indignantly. I began to get up from my desk. "In fact," I added, "I think our little chat is just about over."

"Wait, please, Ms. Fein," Ginsberg said. "I think you misunderstand."

"I think I understand all too well," I said.

"Do you recall Francis X. McMahon on your Paris trip?" Ginsberg asked.

"I certainly do," I replied. "How do you know about him?"

"It's all in your dossier, Ms. Fein," Ginsberg said.

That quieted me down. Francis McMahon was an agent who had neatly duped me into thinking he was the heir to a cognac fortune in France. I'd been acting as an IGO courier at the time. McMahon took me out for a night on the town in Paris, leading me to think he was madly infatuated with me. But it had all been a ruse to get me out of my hotel room for a few hours. While I'd been out gazing gaga at the moon with McMahon, my room was being burglarized and my precious parcel, my reason for being in Paris, was stolen.

And despite all the romantic talk, nothing really happened between me and McMahon. I'd been manipulated. When the "moment of truth" arrived, McMahon had beat a hasty retreat. I had been conned like the rankest of amateurs. But on the other hand, though a great deal was promised, nothing came of it. I considered this for a moment. Then I thought of the arrogant Mr. Alcala, and the idea amused me. Perhaps he could learn that all women wouldn't fall into his arms if he batted his eyes and flexed a muscle or two. I sat back down.

"Tell me more about Alcala, and why you want this swindle worked on him," I requested.

"You have to know about him, Ms. Fein," Ginsberg said as he took a rather thick folder from his attaché case. "He's a rather interesting chap."

"I wouldn't put it quite that way, but let's hear what you have on him."

"Roderigo Alfonso Alcala," Ginsberg intoned. "Born twenty-seven years ago in the Caribbean island republic of El Concepción. Only son of General Marco Alcala, so-called Strong Man of El Concepción, absolute military ruler of that country. Roderigo was educated in the United States." Ginsberg looked up at me and, once he was sure I was paying absolute attention, continued.

"Partly due to his father's strong alliance over the years with the United States and the fact that Roderigo's mother was Margaret Gilbert, the American movie star, Roderigo's ties to our country are strong."

"I know who Margaret Gilbert was," I interjected. "I've seen her films on late-movie programs often. She died some years ago, didn't she?"

"Quite so," Ginsberg said. "An accidental overdose of barbiturates, the reports said. But by then, she was already divorced from General Alcala. Rumor had it that all Alcala had wanted from her was a son and heir. Once Roderigo was born, he had no further use for her."

"The General sounds like a real charmer," I remarked.

"Like father, like son," Case said from his chair. "Fill her in on Roddy's school days, Ginsberg."

"Coming to it, sir," Ginsberg said, and resumed his narrative. "At school, Las Palmas Prep, on the Palos Verdes peninsula, he was involved in several, um . . . romantic escapades with young women there. The girls concerned were bought off to keep silent. Then there was the case of Leon López.

"López was an orphan. His entire family died in a plane crash when they went to attend a relative's funeral in Mexico. López became the ward of an attorney friend of his grandfather's. Although the boy became extremely wealthy from his family's insurance claims, he was straight out of a low-income background in inner city Santa Ana, California. Perhaps to make

López feel more comfortable in his new surroundings, he was made Roderigo's roommate."

"I'll bet that went over big with Alcala," I said.

"We're not quite certain what did happen," Ginsberg said. "But we do know that shortly afterward, López was expelled from Las Palmas. A large amount of marijuana was found concealed under his mattress. The informant was Roderigo Alcala. The other boy swore that the stuff had been planted. And that Roderigo did it." Ginsberg looked up from the dossier for emphasis. "We tend to believe the López story," he added. "On several occasions, Roderigo has publicly demonstrated his absolute contempt for the lower classes, in which he includes anyone who's Hispanic and not rich. This has resulted in his being nicknamed Snotty Roddy by schoolmates. Never to his face, of course."

"I'm amazed none of his school chums have knocked some manners into him," I said.

"That would have been a mistake," Ginsberg said. "Roderigo is a superb athlete, skilled in boxing, fencing, and martial arts. If that weren't enough, almost any place he goes, there are his personal bodyguards, handpicked by the General from the El Concepción Secret Police. They are rough customers, even by Caribbean republic standards. On a par with the former Tonton Macouts of Papa Doc Duvalier of Haiti."

"I didn't see them at the track today," I said.

"They were there, Ms. Fein. You didn't see *me*, either."

"True."

"In any event, Roderigo went on to study at Columbia University in New York. He graduated with honors. He then attended, at his father's insistence, the American War College in Virginia for two years. He holds the commission of major in the El Concepción Air Force. I might add that he's earned his rank."

"I might add that he's earned a swift kick in the pants from someone," I said.

"That may be," Case said, "but it won't come from us."

"I was wondering about that," I said. "Why is the IGO so interested?"

"I'll come to that in due time, Ms. Fein," Ginsberg said. "Shortly after completing his education, Roderigo returned to his native country, and their national security blanket took over. We know very little about the year and a half he lived inside the borders of El Concepción. We know there were rumors of disagreements with his father, but as to the nature of these, we can only speculate.

"About two years ago, a new Roderigo burst upon the public consciousness. He began to establish a national racing team for El Concepción, on the Grand Prix circuit. His country purchased the finest of racing cars, hired the best drivers and mechanics. Pit crews that were the envy of many factory racing teams. And after the first season, they began to win races in a big way. At the present time, Roderigo needs only to win two more major events to be named champion driver of the world. He hopes to win one of them at the Long Beach Grand Prix, this month. Experts say his chances are quite good."

"But why is the IGO so interested in him?" I asked.

"I'll answer that," Case said. "Despite the General's iron grip on his country, there is a guerrilla underground in El Concepción. Quite well organized, and very militant. Snotty Roddy is the heir to the throne, so to speak. And being in the public eye, and outside the borders of El Concepción, he's an excellent target for them. We are trying as best we can to protect him while he's here."

"Wouldn't that be a function of the FBI?" I asked. "It's my impression that the IGO doesn't function inside our borders."

"Don't be naive, Doris," Case said. "This is too big for any one agency. Too important."

"I don't understand," I said. "Granted, we have few countries south of the border that love the U.S.A. I can understand you wanting to avoid any incidents while Roddy is here. But this . . . major operation . . . I can't see the great loss to the world if the 'other side' *did* do something drastic to him. After all, it's their country and their internal politics."

"There is another consideration, Ms. Fein," Ginsberg said, and held up another file folder. "This is a geological survey. It seems there is an excellent chance that some of the largest offshore oil deposits ever discovered are located within the territorial waters of El Concepción."

"I *knew* there had to be something!" I cried in triumph.

"Can you see what could happen if the present regime were overthrown?" Case asked. "For all we know, the guerillas are going to channel all that oil straight to Havana." He coughed behind his hand. "I have no great love for the present government. I fought my war against fascism in Europe. But the present government has been stable for close to thirty years. And they are pro–United States."

"Are you afraid the General won't like us anymore if something happens to Snotty Roddy?" I asked.

"It's more serious than that," Case replied. "A week ago, the General made a top-secret visit to the U.S. Naval Hospital at Bethesda. Ostensibly for a checkup. But the fact is, Doris, that he was there to confirm or deny what his own doctors in El Concepción had told him. Unfortunately, we couldn't give him any better news. He's dying of an inoperable cancer. He has a year, on the outside, to live. That's with radiation and chemotherapy."

"And the heir to the throne is here in California," I said. "Does Roddy know? And does this mysterious 'other side' know, too?"

"I only wish I knew," Case admitted. "The General swore everyone to secrecy about his condition. He said that if the news leaked out that the famed Strong Man no longer ruled with an iron hand, chaos and revolution could break out in El Concepción. Our Latin American political analysts tend to agree."

"So where does Doris Fein fit into all this?"

"Roddy has expressed an interest in you," Case said. "If you were to spend time with him, knowing what you know, perhaps he might let something slip. A casual remark . . . a change in attitude. Anything, no matter how small, can be of help to us."

"This seems rather elaborate for a possible bit of random information," I said, and stared long and hard at Case. "I have the feeling you're not telling me everything. You've never been straight with me in the past. Why should I think so now?"

"For that very reason, Doris," Case replied easily. "In the past, you were greener than grass, easily fooled. After two missions, you've become an experienced operative. I don't think I could fool you if I tried. And I'm not trying. Don't underestimate the value of small bits of information, either. You aren't our only source. We take many small bits and feed them all into an analytic computer. Couple that with the overview of outside data: economic indicators, information from inside Roddy's country . . . hundreds of sources, and a larger picture emerges.

"Also, we have no agent capable of getting inside Roddy's camp. His Secret Police bodyguards see to that. Only a woman, and an attractive one, could get inside Roddy's guard. How's your Spanish, Doris?"

"Not as good as my French," I replied. "I took two years in high school. But it was my second language. I do practice a bit with Jaime Ortega, the sheriff of Santa Amelia. He's a good friend."

"Pero usted puede entender algunas modismos y frases, ¿ no?" inquired Ginsberg in flawless Spanish.

"Yes, I understand idioms and more than a few sentences," I replied in the same language.

"Good," Case said. "Roddy's bodyguards are hardly intellectual heavyweights. He'd speak with them in elementary Spanish. You might overhear something significant to us. Just don't let on that you speak word one of Spanish."

"Gotcha."

"Well, that's it, Doris," Case concluded. "Are you willing to accept the assignment?"

"I frankly don't know. I'd like to think about it."

"No time," Case said. "You have a splendid chance to see him this evening. You have a dinner invitation."

"Omigosh!" I cried, getting to my feet. "Dr. Cane! He's probably been waiting for ages."

"Dr. Cane?"

"My dinner guest," I explained. "Oh, this is dreadful. The poor man." I picked up the phone and buzzed Bruno on the intercom.

"Yes, Ms. Fein?"

"Is Dr. Cane here?"

"Yes, Ms. Fein."

"How long has he been waiting?"

"Just a few minutes, Ms. Fein."

"Give him a cocktail or something and my apologies. Tell him I'll be down soon."

"I did that, Ms. Fein."

"Thank you, Bruno." I quickly hung up. I beat him to it that time. I turned to face the two IGO agents.

"No one can say I don't love my country," I told them. "I may not always agree with her policies. I'm somewhat iffy about this instance."

"We can offer inducements," Ginsberg said.

"What could you offer me?" I said, smiling. "I'm independantly wealthy. I have everything anyone could want."

"I had in mind the gratitude of your government and a presidential citation, Ms. Fein."

I felt my face turning bright red. It's a failing of mine. I blush easily. Ginsberg was right. Although I do have anything anyone could ever want or need, none of it would be possible if I didn't live here in the U.S.A. My whole life style, everything I hold dear, aesthetic and material, could never happen in any other country in the world. I was ashamed of myself for having made my earlier remark.

"I'll do it," I said.

"Then you'll have dinner with Alcala tonight?" Case asked.

"No, but I'll call him. He left a number."

"Don't you think it might be wiser to see him right away?"

"You may know international politics, Mr. Case," I said with a knowing smile, "but you aren't my age. If I call and say I'll see him, that will be enough. He's used to women falling all over him. I'll call him and tell him

I'm not interested in seeing him. Then, when he tries to talk me into seeing him, I'll weaken a bit."

Case made a noise like a laugh. "You *do* have the makings of a born agent, Doris."

"I'm not fond of being devious, Mr. Case," I said. "I know the game and I know the score. I just don't play it. In this case, I'll make an exception. If only to teach Snotty Roddy a lesson." I got up from my desk.

"Your government is most grateful, Ms. Fein," Ginsberg said.

"I doubt if your agency speaks for my government," I said. "And now I have a dinner guest. I'll have Bruno show you out."

Ginsberg reached inside his attaché case again. He came up with more forms I'd seen before. They were IGO contracts, swearing me back into service. Before I left to have dinner with Dr. Cane, I was sworn in and given the necessary phone numbers and code phrases to make my reports.

All through dinner with Dr. Cane, I was preoccupied. I wondered if I had done the right thing. Had I known what lay ahead, I needn't have wondered.

5 / *Just a Shot in the Dark*

"TO THE MOST interesting woman I've met in California," said Roderigo Alcala, raising his glass to me. Oh, brother, I thought, what you need is a longer handle on your shovel. I obligingly nodded and smiled.

We were seated at a table at La Strada restaurant, where I had been treated to an evening of watching Roddy eat things that would have bloated me like a balloon, and hearing him talk about himself, displaying an ego bigger than my dress size at age fifteen.

"Oh, I'm sure you know many fascinating women here, Roddy," I said diffidently.

"But not like you, Doris," he replied. "I was surprised, most pleasantly, when you changed your mind about seeing me."

No more than I was, I thought. I smiled warmly and said, "Professional interest. I've never met a Grand Prix racer, let alone a near-champion."

"And one day, you will compete as well?"

"No, that's not for me. But I have come to appreciate how difficult high-speed driving can be." I sipped at my Perrier. "I used to think it was a terrible waste of money and gasoline. The world is starving for energy, and here are a bunch of grown men burning up gas and rubber to see who can go around a track fastest."

"And now you think differently?"

"I'm still not convinced that all the money and effort couldn't be directed elsewhere. Toward something that could make the world a better place," I said. "However, I *have* come to realize that a driver, must be a real athlete. He has to be in top physical condition and be capable of tremendous concentration."

"True, true," Roddy said, nodding modestly. He polished off the last of his blood-rare New York cut steak. "And one must stay in top shape . . . good diet and such. Did you know that during the Monaco Grand Prix, I lost twelve pounds before the race ended?"

"Money or body weight?" I quipped.

"Weight, of course," Roddy said, missing my joke completely.

"Then I may compete someday, at that," I said. "Jogging can be such a bore."

"And why should you want to lose weight?" Roddie said, elevating an eyebrow and leaning across the table. I think he was giving me his number one facial expression, indicating physical interest.

"Come on, Roddy," I said, "I'm hardly a Vogue model."

"Heaven forbid!" he said with a disdainful look—probably Mild Distaste, # 6. "They are skinny, bloodless creatures with less on their minds than flesh on their bones."

"Is this the voice of experience speaking?"

"I am afraid, so," he said with a rueful shake of his head. "So many people think of me as an empty-headed playboy, toying with race cars, playing at international night spots, without a serious thought on my mind. I am not that way at all, Doris."

"From what I've seen in the newspapers, Roddy, you're doing a good imitation of an international playboy. Are you telling me that you read Proust in your spare time?"

"I have read *Remembrances* and *Swann's Way*," he replied. "But I find Proust rather pallid, though stylish. I prefer your Ernest Hemingway. He understands the Latino way of thinking."

I'll bet you do, I thought. All hairy chest and *machismo.* Aloud, I said: "Really? Which of Hemingway's books?" I expected to hear him cite *The Sun Also Rises* or *Across the River and into the Trees.* To my surprise, he replied, "I think *The Old Man and the Sea* is my favorite. You see, I come from an island republic. My people have been fishermen and farmers for the entire history of El Concepción. They are poor folk. My land has few natural resources, save the fish in our waters and the farmland at the base of our mountains. In Hemingway's book, I can understand so clearly the feelings of the Old Man. He has caught the Great Fish that all fishermen dream of. He will be a hero in his village when he brings that great, beautiful creature into the harbor. Then, with the sharks, Nature takes back the gift she has bestowed on the Old Man. His dreams of glory are chewed to bits with the Great Fish."

"Do you find glory all that important?"

"For myself, personally, no. For my people, yes."

"I don't understand," I said.

"Few people do," Roddy said with a sad smile. "Few non-Latinos, that is. My country is like that Old Man. Poor, held in low esteem by the community of American nations. My countrymen own little, and have little to look forward to. I cannot make them rich. But I can give them a national hero. I can give them the Great Fish I have caught—I can bring home to El Concepción the international driving championship."

"Which they can't eat," I said, "and which will not raise their standard of living or literacy rate. It won't make health conditions any better, either."

"You do not understand the Latino," he said. "Were I to take all the money spent on the racing team and give it to the people of El Concepción, there wouldn't be a fraction of a peso for even half the population. And the current rate of exchange is twelve hundred pesos to your dollar.

"But the championship: that is another matter. Each man, woman, and child could say: 'Yes, I am poor. My country is poor. But my country holds the international driving championship. We have the fastest cars and the best drivers in the world. We are the best at *something.*'

And that, Doris, is beyond any price tag. It is what we Latinos call *amor propio:* self-respect. That is why I race cars. Not for the personal glory, but for my land."

I put down my glass. "You know, Roddy," I said, "I almost believe you. Let me ask you this, though: Would you care if your number two driver was the one to win at Long Beach this month? Your team would have won, but not you personally. Would that be enough?"

"No, I'm afraid not," he said, smiling thinly. "My number two driver is Italian. The economy of El Concepción hardly produces professional drivers. One day, the entire team will be native-born. But now I am the only native-born driver on our team. It must be I who wins. Otherwise, the Great Fish is meaningless."

I smiled inwardly. Roddy had me going for a few minutes. But it seemed his ego was bigger than I'd guessed. He felt that he, and only he, would be able to give his people self-respect and something to be proud of. I suppose he considered himself the self-appointed cultural messiah of El Concepción.

Then I thought of the reason I'd agreed to see Roddy. Of what George Case and Mr. Ginsberg with no first name had told me. "And you feel that this championship is all your people can ever hope for? You are their only chance for the Great Fish?"

"That, too, may change shortly," he said with a strange smile.

"Do tell," I said, leaning across the table.

"I cannot discuss it," he said. "It is a matter of international politics."

"Which would be too much for my poor woman's brain to comprehend?"

"Of course not," Roddy said quickly. "You're trying to bait me with your equal-rights buzz words, Doris Fein. Women have had the vote in El Concepción since our revolution against the Spanish crown almost eighty-five years ago. You cannot say that of the United States. One of our great revolutionary heroes is a woman, María de Córdoba. She was the wife of General de Córdoba. When he fell in battle, she rushed to his side and took up his sword. The ragged army of farmers and fishermen, who were ready to retreat when the General fell, rallied around her. We won the battle. There is a statue to her in our capital city."

He waved at a passing waiter and called for the check. "I do hope you won't insist on paying half of this, will you?" he asked, indicating the bill. I knew the amount would be sizable. La Strada is hardly McDonald's.

"I could pay it all, easily," I said.

"Yes, I know, Doris," he said with a smile. "I know you are extremely wealthy. I know of your holdings, your home, your ownership of a newspaper . . ."

"Say, wait a moment," I said. "I thought I was the one with the reputation for being a snoop. You seem to know an awful lot about me on such short notice."

"Forgive me, Doris. As soon as my . . . er . . . traveling companions knew I was to have this dinner with you, they made certain inquiries."

I felt my face grow warm. "Do you mean to say I've

been investigated? That I had to pass some sort of scrutiny to have dinner with you?"

"Please, Doris, I would do anything not to offend you. But you must understand. I am not simply a wealthy sportsman. I am also a high-ranking member of my government. My father—"

"Is General Marco Alcala, the Strong Man of El Concepción," I said, "leader of the military junta that's ruled your country for thirty years. You are supposed to be next in line to succeed him. Your mother was Margaret Gilbert, the American movie queen. You have three half sisters. Two of them are married to members of your military—"

To his credit, Roddie began to laugh. "Stop, stop," he said, "I surrender. It seems that my companions aren't the only ones who investigate dinner guests."

"You know I own a newspaper," I said. "Don't you think I ever read it?" I waved a hand at the luxurious surroundings. "You see, I must confess to a certain amount of suspicion myself. You've been charming and attentive, but I know what I look like, Roddie. I'm a reasonably attractive, somewhat overweight young woman with thirty million dollars, good teeth, and what some people feel is a good sense of humor. But physically, I'm not the type that drives men mad.

"I inherited all my wealth about a year ago. In no time at all, men who never gave me a second glance when I was plain old Doris Fein were parking their Porsches in my driveway and pleading everlasting, undying love. I was rushed for sororities and invited to parties. Somehow, I couldn't bring myself to believe that a good fairy had turned me into Bo Derek overnight." I got to my feet before Roddy could come around the table and pull out the chair. "When I found out you were well off in your own right, I was curious. Why me? Especially when you've been seen with some of the most beautiful women in the world."

We walked toward the exit and Roddy said, "You may be a very insecure person, Doris. When we first met, you were not impressed with who I am, or my accomplishments. You didn't know who I was, and you didn't care. You were like a tigress in your anger, and none of my supposed charms meant a thing to you. A situation, I might add, that has seldom happened.

"After you drove off, I was intrigued. Here was a woman capable of driving a two-hundred-mile-an-hour Grand Turismo car, and rich enough to own one. I shamelessly bribed your driving instructor for your number."

"You mean Jimmy took money? I have to speak to him."

"Please, don't fault him, Doris. He didn't take money. I impressed him with how sorry I was about the . . . er . . . incident on the track. I told him how I admired his abilities to train a high-speed driver in so short a time, and that I would soon be instituting a driver development program in my country. One that he might be able to design and supervise. . . ."

"And you can't be mad at someone who likes your kid, your dog, or your work," I said.

"Very true," he said, smiling. "Is that remark a Doris Fein original?"

"Wish it were," I admitted. "It was said to me by a very smart old man named Harry Grubb. Years ago."

"Ah yes, your benefactor, according to my informants."

"Don't remind me of your snoopy ways," I said as we waited for the attendant to bring the Red Menace. Roddy had taken a cab to La Strada to meet me. He was staying only minutes away, at the Newporter Inn.

"I won't discuss my snooping, if you don't talk about yours," he rejoined. The attendant brought up the red car and held open the door on the driver's side—for Roddie. I savored the look on his face as I slipped behind the wheel and asked of Roddy, "Give you a lift back to the Newporter?" Roddie looked at the parking attendant and, to his everlasting credit, seemed genuinely amused, too.

"Only if you don't drive too fast, Doris," he said in a wimpy voice. "You know how these fast cars frighten me." He got in on the passenger side and made a big fuss about getting belted in. We both kept straight faces until we'd pulled out of the driveway, then, turning onto the Pacific Coast Highway, we roared with laughter during the short drive to his hotel.

At the front door to the hotel, Roddy got out and asked, "Would you care for a cup of coffee or a brandy at the Palm?" The Palm is an elegant restaurant at the hotel.

I was just about to decline politely when I heard a

sound. It was like a subdued popping, a kid in a school cafeteria stomping on a paper cup. Suddenly, a *verry* large man materialized from out of nowhere. He hurled himself at Roddy and wrestled him to the ground. I looked in my rear-view mirror and saw where he'd come from: a big black Mercedes-Benz that had pulled up behind us when we'd turned into the Newporter. Two other men, clad, like the giant, in dark business suits, hats, and sunglasses, came spilling out of the sedan with pistols in their hands, scanning the adjacent parking lot and shrubbery!

6/ *I've Heard That Name Before*

I GOT OUT of the Red Menace as fast as I could. As I came around the front of the car, I was grabbed by one of the dark-suited men and roughly thrown to the ground.

"Please, very dangerous," the dark-suited man said in my ear, in heavily accented English.

"I've noticed," I said, trying to extricate myself. My action only seemed to encourage him to hold me down more securely. I was getting reconciled to spending the remainder of the evening on the ground in front of the Newporter, when I heard Roddy's voice say in Spanish, "It's all right, Pérez, let her up."

Immediately, the weight was gone. Strong hands helped me to my feet. Roddy was at my side. "Are you all right, Doris?" he asked.

"I'm not sure," I said as I dusted off my beige pants suit. "All the working parts seem to be working." I

61

noted a large tear in the left knee of my suit. "A little ventilation at the knee," I added, "but so far, I'm okay."

"Please, Major Alcala," the huge man said, "can't we go inside?" I almost made a move toward the lobby, but luckily, I remembered what Case had told me. Don't let on you understand a word of Spanish. I waited until Roddy responded.

"Very well, García," Roddie told the giant. Then to me he said: "Shall we go inside, Doris?" He even extended one hand in an "after you" gesture and leaned forward from the waist in a courtly half-bow. If that popping noise was what I thought it was, Roderigo Alcala was some cool customer. Someone had just taken a shot at him, and he was dwelling on social niceties. For all he knew, the gunman was still there, waiting for another shot.

The other dark-suited men had dispersed and were scouring the bushes. As they did, a small, fast car came careening up the drive from the lower parking lot, its headlights turned on high beams. It didn't head for the driveway exit. It was coming toward us!

In an instant, both Roddy and García exploded into action. *"La mujer, García!"* Roddy cried, and from under his well-tailored sports jacket, he produced a small automatic pistol. The wind was knocked out of me as I was again pushed to the pavement. The huge man and Roddy dropped behind the hood of the Red Menace as the racing car came abreast of us. I heard that sound again, and I did my best to get closer to the concrete beneath me. This time, Roddy, and I guess

García, answered the fire. In a few seconds, it was all over.

I was again helped to my feet by García. As he set me upright, I said, "We've got to stop meeting this way, Señor García."

I don't know if he understood me, but in short order, I was hustled inside the lobby. The other men arrived a few seconds later on the run. They exchanged rapid-fire Spanish with Roddy and García. I missed a lot of it, but the upshot was that some *gruperos,* whatever they were, had attacked us. They had made good their getaway, but Roddy felt that he'd hit someone in the car when he'd returned their fire. No one seemed quite clear as to the make of the car or its license number.

All this time, I was sitting in a chair in the lobby, my head going back and forth from speaker to speaker, as though I were watching a tennis match. When the initial flurry of Spanish was over, I said to Roddy, "What's going on? Who are these men? What happened out there?"

"Forgive me, Doris," Roddy said with a thin smile. "I forgot you don't understand." He came over to where I was sitting, and glancing about, saw we were ringed with a crowd of curious hotel patrons. "I can't explain here," he said in a low voice. "Someone's already called the police. Please come up to my suite while there's still time." He paused and smiled. "You'll be quite safe, I assure you."

"Got to be safer than *outside* the hotel, anyhow," I said. The dark-suited men, led by the giant, García, formed a protective circle about us and moved us through the crowd to the nearest elevator. In a few minutes, we were inside what I sincerely hoped was the safety of Roddy's suite. The dark-suited men had preceded us into the rooms, pistols at the ready, and hadn't let us enter until García was satisfied that there were no more surprise guests inside.

Roddy snapped a command in Spanish, and one of the dark-suits went over to the bar and returned with two glasses of brandy. Roddy tossed off his in one gulp. I declined and asked for club soda. After all, it would have been a bit much to ask for Perrier.

"I have to admit," I told Roddy, "dinner with you may be many things. But dull isn't one of them."

"I'm so very, very sorry, Doris," Roddy said. "I had no idea. . . . If I had thought for a second you'd be in danger . . ."

"You make it sound like it rained and you forgot your umbrella," I said. "Roddy, someone just tried to kill us!"

He smiled and spread his hands apart in a typical Latino gesture. "I'm a soldier, Doris," he said. "I am accustomed to being in jeopardy. Unhappily, I am also a key figure in my country's government. I hope you don't think El Concepción is a barbarous land, but one of the risks of being in government is that occasionally, one *does* get shot at. Not all our people are happy with the present government."

"They sure have a nasty way of showing it," I replied. "Whatever became of elections? They're a lot safer than fire fights in a parking lot." Actually, I knew the answer to that one. So-called "free elections" were held in Roddy's land. There was only one candidate for president: General Alcala. Guess who got elected by a landslide?

"We have elections," Roddy replied. "There is one party, however, which is not represented. They are outlawed. Revolutionaries. They call themselves La Grupa de Libertad: the Group for Liberty. Some of them are here in the United States, in exile. My men believe it was their work outside just now."

I nodded. Now I knew what *gruperos* were. Members of La Grupa.

"You knew they have people here, and still you went out to dinner?" I asked. "I mean, forget about *you* for the moment. Surely you knew you were endangering anyone near or with you? They might have used a bomb or something."

"This is the part I don't understand," Roddy answered. "La Grupa has never committed an act of terrorism in this country. They exist in exile by remaining on their best behavior. Any incident of this sort would cause them to lose their political sanctuary. They would be deported to El Concepción. That would be the same as a death sentence. My father is not lenient with his justice."

"I've read that," I said. Roddy's remark was something of an understatement. There are groups of people in this country, Americans, who feel that the regime of General Alcala is as abusive of human rights as some Middle East governments.

"Then why should they suddenly turn on the fireworks?" I asked.

"I don't know," Roddy admitted. "Unless . . ." The puzzled look faded from his face, to be replaced with an expression of sudden realization. Abruptly, he recovered and said to me, "Doris, dear lady, you must excuse me. I must make an emergency telephone call to El Concepción. I also have to explain the shooting incident to the hotel management. They'll be calling the room any moment now. Then there are plans to be made with my men, here. García will see you safely home, if you like."

"Not at all necessary," I said. "In fact, I might be safer from your playmates . . . what did you call them?"

"*Gruperos.*"

"Whatever. I might be better off if I'm not seen with Señor García. He does tend to stand out in a crowd." At this point, I stood up alongside Roddy's bodyguard. He must have towered a foot above me.

"You may be right, Doris," Roddy said, "but I'd never forgive myself if something should befall you."

"I wouldn't take too kindly to it, either," I cracked. "However, I don't think they'll be coming back for an encore. I'm sure the management has called the police by now. They may want to take a statement from me, you know."

"That can be done, if necessary, tomorrow morning, I'm sure," Roddy said.

"You don't put off the police in this country the way

you may in yours," I said. "They have a nasty way of intruding when *they* want to."

"This is no concern of the local police," Roddy said with a wave of his hand. "It is an internal matter, among El Concepción nationals."

"And I suppose I'm an honorary citizen?" I demanded. "One of those bullets may have had your name on it, Roddy. But there were also a few flying around addressed *To whom it may concern.*"

"Ah, but you *were* unhurt," he said with Charming Grin #2.

"Just dumb luck that I wasn't," I answered.

One of the dark-suits said something in Spanish to the effect of "Stop wasting time with this woman. We have business." I kept a lid on my anger. I couldn't acknowledge that I understood. In turn, Roddy became even more charmingly persuasive. He pleaded desolation at the loss of my company, all the while urging me toward the door.

In the end, we compromised. García would see me to my car, and I would drive home alone. The lobby was filled with people and police. I could see a well-turned-out young man, obviously in the employ of the hotel, talking rapidly with some of Newport's Finest. García and I slid by the knot of police and curiosity seekers.

I'd expected that we'd be stopped, but no one pointed a finger in our direction. Then I realized that outside of our little group in front of the hotel, no one had actually witnessed the shooting. The police were still trying to find out what had taken place and who had been involved.

I stood patiently while García made sure there was no one hiding in my car. I was somewhat taken aback when he sprang the hood release of the Red Menace and inspected the engine. He then got down on the ground and examined the undercarriage of the car. He was checking for bombs! He got to his feet and extended one huge paw to me.

"Your keys, *por favor,*" he asked. Puzzled, I gave him my gold key. He waved me back and wedged himself inside and cranked up the engine. It sprang to life with a throaty growl. He got out and held open the door for me. With a sickening realization that he had just put his life on the line, for a stranger, I got inside. Before I pulled away, I leaned out the window and asked, "Mr. García, you were looking for a bomb, weren't you?"

He smiled, displaying a gold tooth. *"No entiendo, señorita,"* he said. "I don't understand."

"Oh, I think you do," I came back. "You just risked your life for me."

"I have orders, señorita."

"And you followed them, no matter what?"

"I am a soldier, señorita," he said with a shrug. Then, he turned and walked toward the lobby. I drove back to my home, considerably shaken. Some intimate dinner date!

Helen Grayson was already asleep when Bruno opened the door for me. I was relieved. Had Helen been awake to see my disheveled state on arrival, I would have spent ages explaining to her what had happened. And even more time assuring her I was unhurt. I *did* have a slight abrasion on my knee, and I knew the slacks to my suit were a total loss. I made my way upstairs, and in a short time was luxuriating in a bubbly tub.

After my bath, and wearing my favorite pink terry robe, I padded down to my study. I was beat to the socks, but I knew that I had to report the events of the wild dinner party to the IGO. I had memorized the twenty-four-hour, toll-free number. As I entered my study, I was surprised to see Bruno behind the desk, his fingers flying over the keys of my computer/processor.

He had the morning and evening editions of *The Register* spread out across the desk and was entering data into the unsolved crime files we keep. Ordinarily, we would have done this together.

"Not sleepy, Bruno?" I asked.

"No, Ms. Fein."

"You can turn in, Bruno," I told him. "I have some calls to make, and after that, I'm off to bed. We can catch up on the files tomorrow night."

He switched off the computer power and got to his feet. He walked toward the door in his eerily silent fashion. Just as he was about to exit, I had a hunch. I called him back.

"Yes, Ms. Fein?"

"Bruno, it may be an off chance, but see if we have anything in our files on Margaret Gilbert. She was a suicide . . . I'd say about twelve years back."

"Our files only go back five years, Ms. Fein."

"Then what makes me think I've seen her name someplace in our files? It may have been in conjunction with a different case."

Obediently, Bruno fired up the computer again and began a cross-index search on Roddy's mother. After a half-hour's scan, he looked up at me. "Nothing, Ms. Fein," he announced.

"Thank you, Bruno," I said. "I must have been mistaken. You can turn in now."

"Yes, Ms. Fein." He shut down the machine and left, making no more sound than one of my Siamese cats crossing the carpet.

I sat behind my desk, still puzzled. Where had I seen the reference to Margaret Gilbert? Then I realized the answer. An understandable mistake. I'd seen her name on a computer printout, all right. It had been on the page of Ginsberg's report on Roddy. Putting it from my mind, I dialed my toll-free number and made my report to the IGO.

I didn't recognize the voice that asked for the identification codes and passwords. I'd hoped that Ginsberg, or Case himself, would be at hand. After hanging up, I trudged wearily to bed. Case had misrepresented the dangers of bogus romance with Roderigo Alcala. I made a mental note to rake him over the coals the next time I had a chance to speak with him.

As I lay in the darkness, that same nagging feeling about Margaret Gilbert returned. I tried to put it from my mind. . . .

7/ Maximilian and Doris?

THE SEAPLANE MADE a graceful loop and landed perfectly on the quiet waters of the tropical lagoon. In a few minutes, I was being assisted from the plane and onto the dock by a tall, thin, distinguished-looking man clad in a white linen suit.

"Welcome, Ms. Fein," he said with a slight Latin accent. "I am Mr. Callahan." He indicated a swarthy dwarf at his side, also wearing a white linen suit. "This is my assistant, De Cal."

"Welcome, señorita," piped the tiny man.

"So happy you could come," Callahan said as we walked ashore from the dock. "Your transportation should be arriving any moment . . . . Yes, here it is, now."

From out of the lush tropical foliage and down the gravel road that led to the lagoon came an elegant nineteenth-century coach of state. Its rich gold fittings

sparkled in the last rays of the sunset. Drivers and footmen in splendid livery, trimmed in golden and silver
threads, sprang into action as soon as the coach came to
a halt. I noted appreciatively the six perfectly matched
gray horses hitched to the luxurious carriage.

One of the footmen rushed to the door of the coach
and let down a small folding step, then threw the door
open wide. Clad in an unbelievably tailored uniform,
suitable for an appearance at the court of Napoleon III,
Roderigo Alfonso Alcala stepped out.

From the top of his plumed fore and aft hat, through
the gold braid epaulets on his shoulders and the jewel-
hilted sword at his side, Roddy was the picture of authority. The footman turned to us and intoned, "His
Imperial Majesty, Maximilian Von Hapsburg: by grace
of God, Emperor of Mexico and all territories of the
Land . . . Defender of the Faith . . ."

The footman fell silent. Roddy had stopped him with
a tiny gesture. "Yes, yes, Pérez, we know all that," he
said airily. His face broke into a ravishing smile as he
approached me. "My dear Carlotta," he said, his arms
extended wide, "it's been an eternity without you. You
must tell me of all the gossip from Paris . . . the affairs
of our cousin Bonaparte . . ." He broke off. "Ah, I see
you have already dressed for your welcoming ball. Is
this the latest style from Paris? All your ladies in waiting
will be green with envy. Greener than the lovely gown
you wear."

I glanced down. My traveling suit had been replaced
with a floor-length gown of emerald-green watered

silk. The skirts ballooned out in the style of the early 1800s. The neckline was cut low, and as I put my hand to my throat in surprise, I could feel the weight of an ornament about my neck. Looking down, what I could see of it on my breast revealed a necklace of exquisite emeralds set with diamonds and platinum. Then I spied my reflection in the glass window of the coach door. I was the model of a *verry* aristocratic lady, right to the elaborate hairdo.

Roddy extended his hand to me.

"Shall we be going, my dear? We have so much to talk about."

The grand ballroom of the palace sparkled with crystal and candlelight, all reflected in the mirrors that lined the great room. The dancers whirled around the floor, forming a respectful circle as Roddy and I waltzed.

"No one dances as you do," he said. "I have yearned these long months to hold you in my arms. Let it be said that even though I be emperor of this land, all my domain means naught. For on this blessed night, I have held an angel in my arms. To compare with this sensation, a crown is mere dross!"

Suddenly from the terrace alongside the ballroom, the sound of gunfire rent the air. Women screamed. The music trailed off into squeaks and faded away. A small band of men, clad in soiled white trousers and shirts open at the neck, came spilling into the brittle beauty of the scene.

All of them wore broad straw sombreros, and bandoliers of rifle bullets crossed their chests. Some were barefoot; all were sporting a week's growth of black stubble on their cheeks. Roddy's hand flew to the sword at his side.

"Touch that blade and you are a dead man, señor," said one of the ragged men in white. The ranks of the intruders opened and the man who had spoken came forward.

He wore the crossed bandoliers; two pistols hung at his sides and a large, evil-looking cane knife, the size of a short sword, was slung across his back, between his shoulders. He had a cigar clenched between his teeth.

"The people of this country will bear your yoke no more, Maximillano," he growled.

It was when he spoke that I recognized the leader of the intruding band of men. It was George T. Case! Sure enough, behind him, in ragged whites, was Mr. Ginsberg, with a drawn pistol aimed directly at Roddy.

"You do not frighten me," Roddy said to Case. "I do not run from rabble."

"Then perhaps you will run from this," Case said with an evil grin. He reached over his shoulder and snapped his fingers. He extended his hand, palm up, to an unseen man behind. In a second, a stick of dynamite was placed in his hand. Case puffed the stump of the cigar into glowing life and touched the short fuse with the redcoaled tip.

"Here. Chew on this, imperial dog!" he shouted and tossed the sizzling fused dynamite directly at us both! I screamed and ducked. In horror, I watched as the dynamite, seemingly with a life of its own, began to roll toward me on the floor. I tried to scramble to my feet, but the elaborate skirts of my ball gown got all tangled up. I fell heavily to the parquetry floor and saw the end of the fuse disappear into the stick of dynamite. It exploded with a—

Rrrrrringg . . . rrrringgg . . . I woke to the insistent telephone at my bedside. Blearily, I checked the time on my alarm clock. It was quarter of six in the morning. I picked up the instrument and said, "Mmmrmph?"

"Doris, this is George Case."

"Good morning, you double-dealer."

"I want to know what you meant in your report. You told the recorder that it was your final report."

"No problem there as to what I meant. Final, as in last. I'm checking out."

"I can't see why."

"You weren't shot at last night. I was."

"The information you gained was extremely valuable, Doris."

"I'm glad. Now can I go back to sleep?"

"Doris, I think you ought to reconsider. Stay on the assignment. It'll only be another few days. After the Long Beach Grand Prix, Roderigo is going back to his country. The matter will be concluded in . . . say, seventy-two hours."

"And what about the chance of *me* being concluded in less?" I asked pointedly. I sat up in bed and yawned expansively.

"I didn't catch that," Case said.

"I didn't say anything. I was yawning. Can't we discuss this at some civilized hour of the day?"

"I've been up for hours."

"And I went to bed at two this morning. Mr. Case, I am bushed. I don't have the strength or energy to argue with you. Call me back in two hours. After breakfast."

"You're not going to your English class at UCI today?"

"How do you know my schedule?"

"We had planned for agent Ginsberg to meet you in the library, after your class."

"How does he get on campus, an outsider? We have security guards to keep strangers out."

"He has a reason. He joined the Friends of the UCI Library. Cost the company all of twenty-five bucks. He can use the library at any time."

"Well, I hope it improves his mind. He can't change mine."

"But you will meet him? There were some details about your report."

"All right, all right, already!" I said. "Anything to get some sleep. I'm not due to get up until eight-thirty. I'll see Ginsberg at eleven, after my English class."

"Thank you, Doris."

"You know, Mr. Case," I said, "that's the first time I've ever heard you say that. A little courtesy goes a long way with me."

"I don't have to thank *professionals* for doing their jobs properly," Case said, and he hung up before I could say any more. I tried to get back to sleep, but his remark about being professional disturbed me. I beat Bruno to the kitchen and was finishing off my glass of Tang when he glided in. In a few minutes, Helen Grayson, fully dressed and ready for the day, came in. She was bright as a new penny. I could have hated her for that, considering how I felt.

But Helen is such a sunny person. For a life filled with tragedy, as hers has been, she always seems to come up smiling. She wanted to know all about my dinner date with Roddy, and my, wasn't he a handsome chap.

"How do you know that?" I asked. "I met him at the hotel."

"Haven't you seen this morning's paper?" she asked, and handed me the paper.

There was an entire supplement on the Long Beach Grand Prix. Diagrams of the race course itself, which is run over the city streets of Long Beach, near the waterfront, and biographies of the various drivers. Principal among them was a half-page photo of Roddy. He was pictured in the winners' circle at a Grand Prix in Belgium. He had a trophy on one arm and the current Miss Universe on the other. She was pouring champagne into the big cup he'd won. I viewed the photo with a jaundiced eye. Miss Universe made me look like a guy. A rather pudgy one, at that.

"Yes, he looks handsome," I agreed. "But Helen, if you keep showing me pictures of women like that, you won't help my morale a bit."

"Is that a bid for a compliment, Doris?" she asked with a smile. "I've never noticed that you lack for male attention. In fact, while you were out to dinner, that nice Dr. Cane called. Thanked you for the . . . how did he put it? *Knockout dinner,* I believe he said." She gave me a puzzled look. "I presume that's a compliment? I'm somewhat out of touch with the way young people express themselves these days."

"It was a compliment, Helen," I said, and added: *"These* days we express ourselves differently? I'm sure that when you were in your teens, people thought you spoke a foreign language, too. Every generation has its slang, its fads and idols.

"To my generation, *knockout* means something great. Like, it was so good it knocked me out. That could change, too. I remember when *bad* actually meant good. Now it means what it used to."

Helen smiled, evidently remembering her teens. "Oh yes, we had our slang: 'cooking with gas' . . . 'a square from Delaware' . . . so many things; I've forgotten most of them."

"Did you used to swoon over Frank Sinatra, or was it Rudolph Valentino?" I asked.

"Neither one," Helen replied. "My generation went gaga over Clark Gable."

"You weren't the only generation," I said. "He was a superstar for decades. Until he died, in 1960. He was still attractive and a leading man at sixty years of age."

"Men can do that," Helen said. "For a woman, once you pass a certain age, you end up playing someone's mother."

"Oh, I don't know about that," I countered. "Look at Marlene Dietrich and Katherine Hepburn. They played lead roles; romantic leads into their fifties."

"And look at all the poor women who couldn't do that. Some even committed suicide when they couldn't get romantic roles anymore."

Something clicked in my mind. It had been bothering me for a while, and Helen's remark about suicides brought it all back. "Helen," I asked, "do you remember Margaret Gilbert?"

"Oh my, yes," she replied. "A beautiful creature, she was. At one time, people used to say I resembled her. Naturally, I was much younger then."

"How much do you remember about her, Helen?"

"Quite a bit. When people tell you that you look like someone, you tend to take more interest. Of course, she's dead, poor thing. Another of those suicides. She'd been a world beauty for twenty years when she died at only thirty-seven. The papers said she wasn't getting the starring parts anymore, and that's what drove her to suicide.

"I used to follow her career. Not just in the newspapers, either. I must confess I read about her in *Modern Screen* and *Photoplay*, too."

"Why, Helen!" I said, stunned. "You used to read *fan* magazines?"

"Back then, almost everyone did. Really, Doris, I was an ordinary young woman, like anyone else." She put her hand to her hair. "I think I've weathered the years well, too."

"Now who's fishing for compliments?" I asked and watched her blush. Helen would blush for card tricks. They say that it's beneficial to the complexion. I can believe it. At her age, Helen has exquisite skin.

"Tell me," I continued, "what you know about Gilbert."

"Let me see. . . . She was born in Beaumont, Texas. Broke into the movies about thirty years ago. She was married three times. Once to your young man's father. . . ."

"He's not my young man, dear. We had dinner, that's all."

"Whatever. Then she married Alan Taylor, the playwright, and finally that football player . . . George Garibaldi. She was divorced when she died."

"Any children, other than Roddy?"

"Why, yes, a daughter. She'd be about . . . twenty-one years old, I should say. That was her marriage to Taylor, the playwright."

"That's it!" I cried in triumph.

"That's what?" she asked, totally mystified.

I came around the breakfast table and kissed her on the cheek. "You are a sweet, helpful person, Helen," I said. "Now I have to run upstairs. Do be a dear and ring Bruno for me, won't you? Tell him to meet me in the study in a half-hour."

"But what did I do? Or say?"

"Just resolved something that's been nagging at the back of my mind for a day now. I'll explain later."

An hour later, after Bruno had shut down the computer, I had my answer. And I had an earful to lay on agent Ginsberg when I saw him. I rushed to the garage and in a few minutes was making the short drive to UCI.

8/ Speedy Ginsberg

I SAW AGENT Ginsberg before he saw me. I'd entered
the library from a lower floor. He was on the first,
checking out the main entrance and, I suppose, watching for me. He had an opened book on the table in front
of him. Camouflage, I was sure, but I couldn't resist
coming up behind him to see what the title was. He was
"reading" Kurt Vonnegut's *Player Piano.*

"Feeling anti-company this morning, agent Ginsberg?" I asked.

He gave a small start and spun around in his chair. "I
beg your pardon?" he said.

"The book you're reading," I explained. "It's *verry*
anti-establishment.

He glanced down at the novel. "It was on the table
when I got here," he said. "I was just thumbing through
it."

Ginsberg had shed his IGO East Coast uniform of

dark suit, light shirt, and striped tie. He was clad in a mauve polo shirt, white jeans, and Adidas. He looked years younger than when I'd first seen him in my study.

"Seems suspicious to me," I kidded, "reading subversive fiction and dressing Southern California. Next thing you know, you'll be buying a surfboard and eating at fast-food chains. Mr. Ginsberg, I think you're going native."

He smiled broadly: something I hadn't seen him do in George Case's company. But then again, I rarely smile when Case is on the scene, either. He gives one so little to laugh about.

"It wouldn't be the first time an agent went native," Ginsberg said. "In my case, it's reversion to type, Ms. Fein. I was born in Santa Barbara."

"Funny, I would have pegged you for an easterner."

"It was the suit, I think. I'd been recently called in from Maryland for this case. Being a native, and all. That, and the fact that I'm bilingual and have lived in Central America."

"There would appear to be more to you than surface, Mr. Ginsberg," I said, sitting down next to him at the table. "And by the way, I can't keep calling you Ginsberg or Mister. You do have a first name, don't you?"

"I do, indeed," he said with a smile. "Michael."

"Do your friends call you Mike?"

"No, oddly enough. Most of my old school pals call me Ginsberg. Or Speedy."

"Speedy? You've got to be kidding. Speedy Ginsberg?"

"Track team at Stanford. The name stuck."

"Okay, Speedy it is." I leaned across the table and pointed to a paragraph in *Player Piano*. Pure decoy. I said in a low voice: "I have a lead on who took those shots at Snotty Roddy last night. In fact, I've come up with a whole new angle on the matter. It wasn't in my last-night's telephone report. It fell into place this morning."

"You seem to have had a change of heart, Ms. Fein."

"Doris."

"Doris, then. I was under the impression you were bowing out of the investigation."

"I was. Then I discovered some fascinating background on Roddy. Or, more properly, his sister."

"Alcala has no sister."

"His half sister, Estelle Taylor."

"Oh yes," Ginsberg said. "Margaret Gilbert's daughter by her marriage to Alan Taylor. By the way, she goes by Estelle Tuchman. That's Alan Taylor's real name. Taylor is his pseudonym."

"Then you know about her revolutionary activities?" I asked, somewhat disappointed. I thought I'd come up with something the IGO had missed.

"It's more an FBI matter," Speedy Ginsberg replied. "When one of her group took a shot at a federal judge two years ago and fled the country, it was suspected that Tuchman helped him escape. She was subsequently cleared. We don't have an active file on her. Last I heard of, she was living in Cambridge, Massachusetts, with her father."

"Think again, Speedy," I said in triumph. "She's right here in Southern California."

"You're certain? You've seen her?"

"Sort of. If you'll come with me, so can you."

I led Speedy Ginsberg downstairs to the section of the UCI library where they keep microfilm copies of most major newspapers. We set up one of the microfiche projectors, and I screened *The Register* from a week before. It took me a few minutes to find what I was looking for. My own machine at home is newer and quicker.

"Here it is," I said.

It was a photo of a group of protesters outside the Federal Building in the Westwood section of Los Angeles. They were a typical group of activists: work clothes, jeans, beards, and picket signs. The placards read: NO HUMAN RIGHTS IN EL CONCEPCIÓN, ALCALA MURDERS HUNDREDS WITH U.S. HELP, and most frequently, NO MILITARY AID TO ALCALA!

"That's her, right there," I said, pointing to a young woman in the crowd. She was about twenty-one, short, and a bit heavyset, though that could have been the army surplus fatigues she wore. Her hair was shoulder length. She may have been pretty, but her features were distorted by emotion. It seemed the camera had caught her in mid-shout. The caption read:

Protesters of Alcala regime picket Federal Building. About fifty members of the Free El Concepción Federation, among them, Estelle

*Tuchman, daughter of Pulitzer playwright
Alan Taylor, assembled at Federal Building.
No arrests were made.*

The story went on to say that the protest group was
collecting funds to aid political refugees from El Concepción and sending medical supplies to insurgents in
the mountain provinces of that country. Several celeb-
rities had lent their names and donated money. In that
paragraph, the writer further identified Estelle as Margaret Gilbert's daughter as well as Alan Taylor's.

"Interesting," Ginsberg said.

"That's all? Just interesting?"

"What would you have me say? Yes, she's Roddy's
half sister. I've heard of heavy sibling rivalry, but taking
a shot at your brother *is* a bit much, don't you think?"

"So is a wing shot at a federal judge," I countered,
"and she was up to her neck in that affair. Radicals tend
to stay radicals."

"Oh, I don't know. I've seen a few turn up lately
saying that they've found God and have mended their
ways."

"Estelle doesn't seem too sanctified in her picture
there," I said, indicating the photo on the microfiche.
"And this time, her cause is too close to home to be a
coincidence. She's after Roddy and his father.

"And there's more. Alan Taylor, when he wrote the
play about his dead wife—"

"*The Poor Goddess?*" Ginsberg said. "I saw it. Not
first-rate Alan Taylor, I'm afraid."

"Yes, but you'll recall that in the play, he showed that the path to Margaret Gilbert's suicide began when General Alcala rejected her. He made it pretty clear that Gilbert's dreadful emotional insecurity turned to self-destructiveness after the General divorced her. And for alleged infidelity, at that."

"It was the only grounds he could have used," Ginsberg said. "El Concepción is a Catholic country."

"But what if all this preys on Estelle's mind?" I persisted. "She probably blames her mother's death on Roddy's father, and indirectly on Roddy himself. She has radical connections, a past history of being involved with violence and gunplay, and to my way of thinking, a pip of a motive for wanting Roddy dead."

Speedy Ginsberg stood up and switched off the projector. He rewound the spool and we replaced it in its proper file cabinet. As we waited for the elevator to the main floor, he said, "Case was right about you, Doris. You have the makings of a first-rate agent."

"George Case said that about me?"

"Among other things."

"Do tell. What other things?"

"You wouldn't care to hear."

"On the contrary. I'll make a scene in the elevator if you don't tell me."

The elevator arrived and the car was empty. "No one to overhear us, Speedy," I said. "Let's hear Case's critique of Doris Fein."

"Very well. He said you are chronically inquisitive and have a high degree of intuitive aptitude for investigation. That you are headstrong, undisciplined, too emotional, and don't take orders well. Most of all, and most important so far as Case is concerned, you lack the proper attitude toward authority."

"Is he trying to say he don't get no respect from me?" I asked in my best Rodney Dangerfield impression.

"I think so."

"You were dead wrong about my feelings," I said as we left the elevator and walked out the main library entrance. "If that's George Case's impression of me, I'm delighted."

"That may be, but there's still the matter of your leaving the investigation. Based on that, I was to do a debriefing on you. We haven't done it. Can I assume you're still on the case?"

"Tell you what," I said as we approached the student parking lot. "If I have no further contact with George Case, I'll do it."

"That's no problem, Doris. He's back in Maryland right now. I'll be running you as an agent. You'll report to me."

"Then you got a deal, Speedy," I said, getting into the Red Menace and firing up the engine.

"Nice car," Speedy Ginsberg noted.

"I'll give you a ride sometime."

"I may take you up on that, once this job is over. I have some rest and recuperation time due. I was going to visit my folks in Santa Barbara. The company's saved me airfare with this assignment." He glanced at his

watch. "I have to call in, myself. To Case, personally."
He made a small grimace.

"I don't think you like him any more than I do," I
said.

"I don't think it matters whether I do or not," Speedy
replied. "He's the boss, and that's it. Now, don't forget,
Doris. Anything Roddy says can be important. Should
he get in touch with you again, see him."

"That may be hard to justify. Anyone who's been
shot at wouldn't do it. What's my reason, O master
spy?"

"Probably that he's the most fascinating man you've
ever met. If his ego's as large as his dossier indicates,
he'll believe it in a flash."

"I hate to say it, but I think you're right."

I backed out of my parking spot, waved a good-bye
to Speedy Ginsberg, and buzzed out onto Campus
Drive toward the freeway. I punched the tape deck
control and motored home to Chopin's *Nocturnes,*
played by Novaes.

I had a surprise awaiting me at home. When Bruno
let me in, I discovered that the foyer of my house was
filled with floral displays, all huge, all *verry* expensive,
and all blood-red roses.

"Aren't they lovely?" commented Helen Grayson.
"There are more in the sitting room and the drawing
room. They're from Señor Alcala."

"Lovely?" I quipped. "The place looks like Forest
Lawn!"

"In the language of flowers, red roses stand for true love," Helen said.

"In the language of Floral Express, I'd say they stand for close to a thousand dollars," I replied. "Any message with them?"

"There's a card on the table over there."

"What does it say?"

"Doris! I'd never read someone else's *billet-doux.*"

I went over to the marble-topped table and picked up the card in the envelope. Helen Grayson went into the music room. Just as I was opening the envelope and she was closing the door, she called out: "He wants to have dinner with you. Privately."

"Helen!"

"Well . . . the envelope wasn't sealed."

I went into my office and dialed Roddy's hotel. He was out, seeing to preparations for the Grand Prix. I should have known he would be. But frankly, the events of last night had driven the race from my mind. Not so Roddy Alcala. He might be many things, but chicken isn't one of them, I thought. He was going to race tomorrow, despite the attempt on his life!

I wouldn't have done it. The Long Beach Grand Prix is watched by thousands from grandstands, but almost as many view the race from terraces on apartment buildings on Ocean Avenue. Any window overlooking the race course—and there are thousands—could harbor a sniper with a high-powered rifle.

And there's no question of security. In a situation not unlike the one in which President Kennedy died in

Dallas, there's just no way to cover all the places a sniper could hide. No matter what I thought of Roddy personally, I couldn't let him do it without weighing the risks. I had to talk to him.

Bruno hadn't put away the Red Menace. I changed into my driving suit and soon was nudging fifty-five miles per hour toward the Long Beach Freeway. In a few minutes I was in downtown Long Beach, in sight of the *Queen Mary.* The beautiful old Cunard ocean liner has been converted into a museum and hotel. It's become a Long Beach landmark. The race course runs right along the waterfront, and the gracious old lady of the seas forms a colorful backdrop.

The stands were already erected and most sections of the course closed to ordinary traffic. That was done to allow practice laps for the drivers. I got through security to the pits area with my press credentials from *The Register.* A guard directed me to where the El Concepción race team was assigned. As I parked and began walking toward the pits, I saw Roddy's McClaren pull out onto the race course and accelerate at a frightening rate. I waved to him, but he didn't see me.

The incredibly powerful machine roared down the short straightaway and into the first curve. I'd estimate he was already turning over a hundred miles an hour as he thundered into the turn. Then it happened. His inside front tire seemed to disintegrate off the rim. The car slued sideways, caromed off the barrier, and exploded in a hellish ball of flame!

9/ *Caught Red-Handed!*

I BEGAN RUNNING toward the fiery scene. I called out Roddy's name as I did. Foolish of me. The wreckage was many yards away. Fire trucks materialized and an ambulance dashed down the roadway past me. I was still a hundred yards from the crash when I was grabbed from behind by strong hands. I spun around and found myself face to face with Roderigo Alcala!

"But how . . . ?" I began.

"It wasn't I at the wheel, Doris," he said over the wailing sirens of the emergency vehicles. "Another team driver . . . Nino Locassio, the Italian I told you of." He shook his head as he looked toward the flames. "Accidents do happen, but one never gets used to them."

"That was no accident," I said, and I told him about the way the car's tire had gone to pieces.

"You're quite certain?" he pressed.

"No doubt of it."

92

"Please come with me, Doris," he said, taking my elbow and walking back toward the pit area.

"But aren't you going . . . there?" I asked, indicating the mangled car, now smoldering under a coating of chemical foam being applied by the fire equipment.

"Nothing we can do but pray for Locassio," Roddie replied. "We'd only be in the way right now. Please come with me, Doris."

I went back to the pit area, where Roddy had a hurried discussion in rapid-fire Spanish and almost as fluent Italian with the staff of mechanics that made up his racing team. It was then I saw the other McClaren car, untouched.

I should have known there was another car. I knew the El Concepción racing team had to have more than one car; you couldn't call it a team otherwise. But somehow, after the incident at the hotel last night, I'd assumed the driver had been Roddy. Evidently, so had whoever caused the "accident." Roddy saw me looking over the car.

"This is no time to raise such a subject, Doris," he said, "but I find it touching that you were concerned. You thought I was at the wheel, didn't you?"

"Sure did."

"It would have been me, you know," he said. "I asked Nino to take my car out. It had been acting a bit oddly during acceleration. Nino isn't just a driver. He knows cars well. I thought perhaps he . . ." His voice trailed off. The phone in the pit rang and he sprinted to answer it. I couldn't hear the conversation, but when he came back to where I stood, he was smiling. Grimly, but smiling, nonetheless.

"Good news," he announced. "Nino is alive. He's badly injured and burned, but he is alive. He's being taken to a trauma and burn center."

As if on cue, an emergency helicopter began to descend over the track where the wreck had been. We saw the various emergency personnel scramble out of the path of the chopper, then converge again once the aircraft had landed.

"They'll probably be taking him to Kaiser," I said. "It's not far from here. Do you want me to drive you over there?"

"That would be marvelous," he said. "You are a kind person, Doris Fein."

"Anyone with a scrap of humanity would do it," I disclaimed. "Come on. My car is over there."

We waited for a small eternity in the corridor of the hospital. Fortunately, we were allowed to wait in privacy. Downstairs, in the lobby, there was a small army of press and TV reporters. We had come through the lobby to the accompaniment of a fusillade of flashbulbs and questions. I spotted John Perry of *The Register* in the group, his camera firing away. He came toward us, but I waved him off. He got my unspoken message. Not so the rest of the representatives of the Fourth Estate. They may be my colleagues, but sometimes they act more like vultures.

A man in surgical greens came down the hall. He

spotted Roddy, who was still wearing his aluminized driving suit with his team insignia on it. I was wearing a similar outfit. The man came over to us.

"Are you Mr. Alcala?" he asked Roddy.

"Yes, yes," Roddy said quickly. "How is Nino?"

"Resting now, but not good," the doctor said. "The burns are serious. Over thirty percent of his body. The other injuries are serious as well. But while he was conscious, he kept asking that you be given a message, Mr. Alcala."

"What did he say?"

"That's the problem, sir. He spoke in Italian, and I didn't know what he was saying. He just kept repeating your name."

"Can I see him?"

"I'm not sure. He's been given a great deal of medication for the pain. He may not be conscious."

"It's most important, Doctor . . ."

"Wilson. Max Wilson."

"Dr. Wilson, some unusual things have been happening since my team arrived in California. What Nino says may have a bearing on those events."

"Very well, Mr. Alcala. If he's coherent, you can have five minutes with him. But no more." Wilson looked at me. "You'll have to go alone, Mr. Alcala. Unless this is your driver's wife."

I nodded at Roddy, as if to say, "That's all right." Aloud I said, "I'll wait here, doctor. I'm just a friend of Mr. Alcala's."

In almost exactly five minutes, Roddy returned. His face was grim. I had a million questions to ask of him, but Dr. Wilson was still with him. They had a quiet conference I couldn't overhear; then Roddy rejoined me.

"What did Nino say?" I asked as soon as we were alone.

"He was semidelirious from drugs," Roddy said softly. "I managed to get what he meant, though. He said what you told me on the way over here. That the tire seemed to explode off the rim.

"I've seen tires break down under the heat and strain of racing. But the car was only into the first turn when this happened. And when tires let go, there's some sort of warning sign first. I have a terrible suspicion, Doris. I know of just one thing that could cause what you and Nino described."

"Tell me, for goodness' sake."

"An explosive rifle bullet," he replied ominously.

We managed to avoid the waiting press corps by taking a side entrance from the hospital. Halfway to the Red Menace, we were spotted in the parking lot. We were hardly inconspicuous in our Martian-style driving suits. We ran the rest of the distance to my car and got out of the parking area briskly.

"A real Le Mans running start," Roddy commented as we turned onto the San Diego freeway. "You run well, Doris."

"I'm in shape," I replied as we buzzed down the

freeway. "I recently spent some time at Aphrodite's."

"I've heard of the place," Roddy commented. "There are many international stars who go there."

I chose not to tell him that Aphrodite's was no longer in business, mostly due to my efforts. The spa had put me in great condition, as they'd promised. They'd also given me a temporary dependence on amphetamines, and I'd nearly been drowned in an electrified swimming pool as well. But that was history now.

"May I ask where we're going?" Roddy inquired.

"I thought to my place," I said. "There are bound to be a slew of reporters at your hotel by now. You can call your 'traveling companions' from there and have a change of clothes sent over. If you like, I can have Bruno whip up a meal."

"I don't think I could eat a thing," Roddy said.

"Of course," I said quickly, "just thought I'd offer." As I said the words, I heard a low growl from Petunia. I realized then that I'd gone directly from home after my meeting with Speedy Ginsberg and then on to the race course without a bite of lunch. I glanced at the digital clock on my dash. It was five-thirty.

True, I felt compassion for the poor driver lying there in the hospital. And I understood and sympathized with Roddy. But I'm afraid that my alter ego, Petunia Fein, has no conscience whatever. She's the sort of person who, if shown Leonardo's *Last Supper*, would wonder what the menu was for that event.

I was about to change lanes when the black Olds

sedan appeared in my rear-view mirror. It was closing the distance between us rapidly. At first, I thought it was another curious driver trying to make out the brand name of my car. But something felt subtly wrong.

Usually, the cars that come close for a look are other sports cars. Their drivers are always interested in such exotic transportation as the Red Menace. But this was a four-door sedan, looking like it came from a U-Drive agency.

"Roddy, what make of car do your bodyguards drive? A Mercedes, isn't it?"

"Yes, a six-passenger. Why?"

"Look behind us. That Olds is coming up fast."

He swung around in the seat and looked at the black car, now hardly more than twenty feet behind us. "I hope, my dear Doris," he said, "that you have learned your lessons well at the racetrack. The driver of that car is someone I recognize. Can you get us away from him quickly?"

"Try this," I said as I downshifted and gunned the engine. As I engaged third gear at slightly better than half throttle, the rear tires chirped on the concrete road. In a matter of seconds, the black car had retreated in my rear-view mirror to toylike dimensions. I checked my speedometer and discovered to my shock that I was doing 115 miles per hour. In third gear!

I quickly eased up on the gas pedal and with an artful braking maneuver, if I must say so myself, exited from the freeway. I took side streets and roads from there to my house in Santa Amelia. The Rovers were there to greet me, and I had to let them know Roddy was approved company. Bruno let us into the house.

"Your home is beautiful, Doris," Roddy said appreciatively as he walked with me to the downstairs sitting room. "So are your guard dogs. I presume they are attack-trained."

"They certainly are," I said. "They were already trained when I got them. Or, I should say, inherited them."

"Ah yes, the man who left you his fortune. You must tell me about that one day."

"I will, if either of us survives our relationship, Roddy. You know, I think that socializing with you can definitely be hazardous to a girl's health."

"Forgive me for my lack of consideration, Doris," he said. "You have behaved so . . . professionally in these trying circumstances. I have treated you as I would a trained diplomat or even an intelligence agent of my country. You are a remarkable woman . . ." He broke off and put a palm to his forehead.

"What's wrong?" I asked.

"My men . . . García and Pérez and the others. They don't know where I am. They must be turning the hospital upside down to find me." He indicated the antique French phone on a nearby table. "May I?" he asked.

"Of course," I replied. "Dial nine first, then your number. I'll give you some privacy. I have to change clothes anyhow."

I left the room before he picked up the receiver, and sprinted to the nearest extension, on the staircase landing between the first and second floors. I timed it perfectly. As I picked up the receiver, he was still dialing. I hoped that the dial sounds covered the subtle tick that my listening in had caused.

If I'd expected an earful of new information, I was to be disappointed. He got through to his hotel and rang his suite. The man called Pérez answered. The fast-moving Spanish conversation was too much for me to follow, except in general terms. But nothing earth-shaking, for all that. He ordered that García be sent over with his change of clothing, told Pérez to stay near the phone, and gave some other orders for his dark-suited minions that I couldn't catch. Then he said to Pérez: "*Momentito. Espérase . . .*" which means "Just a minute. Hold on."

I'd supposed that he was looking for something to write a message with. Or he was making sure of his privacy in the sitting room. I leaned forward, as though doing so would let me hear better. I nearly jumped out of my skin when I felt a hand on my shoulder. I whirled and found myself face to face with Roderigo Alcala.

"The charade is over, Doris," he said firmly. "I think we must have a talk, don't you?"

10/ A Nasty Surprise

"I DON'T KNOW what you're talking about," I lied. "I was going to make a call. I wasn't sure if you were finished with your conversation, that's all."

"You insult my intelligence," Roddy said.

"And you abuse my hospitality," I countered. "I don't like being called a liar." Especially when I'm lying through my teeth, I thought.

"I don't know where the truth of this matter is," Roddy said grimly, "but I intend to find out. Right now."

I really shouldn't lie. I don't do it well; it goes against everything I've been raised to respect. I had taken this assignment partly because of patriotism and partly because my pride in myself as a woman was offended. All studied machos and so-called "ladies' men" offend me.

However, little by little, a grudging respect for Roderigo Alcala was growing in my mind. That's what made the lying so hard. But I was determined to brazen things out, despite the fact that I'd been caught red-handed, listening in on his conversation.

"I really must get dressed," I said, and moved to go upstairs. Roddy grabbed my wrist. I froze instantly and in my chilliest manner said, "Do you mind? I don't allow myself to be pawed."

"And I don't allow myself to be duped," Roddy retorted, not loosening his grip. I was beginning to get a bit panicky. This so-charming fellow could be dangerous. His father's reputation for interrogating political prisoners was well known. For all I knew, it ran in the family. Then I saw Bruno coming up the stairs. He must have heard the angry voices.

Roddy's back was to Bruno, and knowing how eerily silent Bruno is in motion, I was sure Roddy hadn't noticed. In a flash, I remembered what Speedy Ginsberg had said in his report on Roddy. That he was a superb athlete and skilled in martial arts. I didn't want Bruno getting hurt. I had to warn him somehow.

"What will you do now?" I demanded of Roddy, "use some of your karate on me? Maybe jujitsu? I know you can break bricks with your hands." Did I see a flicker of acknowledgment on Bruno's face? I couldn't be sure.

He moved up the stairs like a shadow and, without a word, clipped Roddy at the back of the neck. Alcala fell like a tree hit by lightning. He would have tumbled down the stairs from the second-floor landing where we stood. But Bruno caught him up in his massive arms and stood there with no more expression on his face than if he were taking out the trash.

"Shall I throw him out, Ms. Fein?" Bruno inquired.

"No, no. Bring him downstairs and put him on the big couch in the sitting room," I said. "Did you hurt him badly, Bruno?"

Without a further word, Bruno shifted Roddy's weight to one arm. I marveled silently at the man's immense strength. With his free hand, Bruno peeled back one of Alacala's eyelids.

"I don't think so, Ms. Fein," he said. Then he walked down the stairs and carried Roddy into the sitting room. I followed. He set Roddy down gently and glided out of the room. In a few seconds he returned with a small silver bowl filled with ice and a sparkling damask napkin on a tray.

I took the napkin and, wetting it, dabbed at Roddy's face. In a few seconds, his eyelids began to flicker. He regained consciousness with a rush and tried to leap to his feet. Bruno restrained him from behind with one massive hand.

"I wouldn't try jumping around, Roddy," I advised. "Bruno might misunderstand your intent. As you've learned, he's quite strong." I could have added, as *I've* just learned. I'd never seen Bruno do anything more menacing than serve dinner. Roddy looked over his shoulder at Bruno with respect written all over his face.

"I underestimated you, Ms. Fein," Roddy said. "In whose employ are you? Now that you have me, what do you want? Money?"

"Don't be absurd, Roddy. I'm rich."

"Then you're one of those living-room radicals, taking up causes you know nothing about." His voice dripped contempt.

"You're right in one sense," I replied. "I don't know what you're talking about, cause or no cause. But don't think you're being detained. I wouldn't touch you with a cattle prod, Señor Alcala. I have no use for anyone who'd manhandle a woman. As soon as your man gets here with your clothes, you're free to go. And I never want to see you again. Bruno did what he did because he thought I was in physical danger. So did I."

Roddy's expression softened. He leaned back in the sofa. "I'm sorry, Doris," he said wearily. "I overreacted. You can't know the strain I've been under. It's not just the race and the driving title . . ."

"I'd hardly think your competition in the race would try to kill you," I replied drily.

"Things at home are getting terribly complicated," he said tiredly. "You wouldn't understand."

"I understand a lot more than you think I do," I snapped. "I'm no follower of radical chic, either. I read my own newspaper and two others, each day. I'm not politically unaware, Roddy. My financial advisers keep abreast of all changes in this hemisphere where I have investments. I get weekly reports."

"You'd hardly get reports on this matter."

"Oh really?" I said, not being able to resist shaking him up a bit. "You mean I know nothing about the geological survey? And your precious offshore oil deposits? The Great Fish, indeed!"

It had the effect I'd hoped for. It was as though all the air had been let out of him. Suddenly, he looked like a kid whose dog had died. My impulse was to sit down beside him, but darn it, I was mad. I could still feel his grip on my wrist. I glanced down and saw the red imprints where he'd grabbed me.

We stayed that way, facing each other for what seemed like a small eternity. I was about to speak again when we heard the front gate buzzer. Bruno looked askance at me.

"It's all right, Bruno," I said. "That would be Señor Alcala's men with his change of clothing and his car. If it is, let them in." I looked at the deflated Roddy. "I don't think we have to worry about Mr. Alcala anymore. Do we, Roddy?"

Roddy made a weary gesture with his hand, as if to say, "I've had it." Bruno left the room. Roddy and I sat in silence until we heard the front door bell. I could hear the conversation from the hall. Bruno came into the sitting room alone.

"Mr. Alcala's party is here, Ms. Fein."

"I'll be right out," Roddy said. Bruno left without a word.

"Well, this is good-bye, Roddy," I said, and didn't extend my hand. I wasn't about to walk him out, either.

"I suppose so," Roddy said. "And I suppose my apologies wouldn't mean anything?"

"Not one bit. Good-bye, Roddy."

"Good-bye, Doris," he said. "One day, I shall write a letter to you. I'll be able to say things I couldn't these past few days. I hope you'll read it."

"Try me."

He walked slowly to the sitting room door, closing it silently behind him. I heard some voices through the door: a few sentences in Spanish. I caught the phrase "We are armed." Hmmm. Things were heating up. Roddy's men were ready to shoot at anything, it seemed. I made a mental note to include that information when I called Ginsberg. Then the darndest thing happened. Roddy raised his voice and said quite clearly in French, of all things, "Doris, these are not my men. If you care about me, call my hotel. García is my man. Trust no one else!"

I hurried to the foyer. Roddy was just being hustled into the back of the black Olds sedan we'd seen on the freeway. The door closed and the sedan began to move. Too late. Besides, I knew those men were armed. Even Bruno's great strength would have done no good against bullets.

"Quick, Bruno," I cried. "Lock the gate! Don't let them through!"

"Yes, Ms. Fein," he said and raced toward the controls to the big iron gates that seal off my driveway from the street. I dashed out onto the lawn and whistled up the Rover Boys. They came racing across the grass.

"Strangers!" I cried, which was their attack cue. "Go

get 'em, boys!" The two Alsatians immediately tore off after the retreating car. I ran in pursuit.

We were too late. The gates close slowly, and were still fairly wide apart as the black Olds raced down the last stretch of driveway. They didn't get through, quite. The left front end of the car hit the gate with a resounding crash, but the car proceeded, leaving the section of gate hanging and useless. In a moment, all I could see was the red trace of taillights disappearing down the street. I suddenly knew what I had to do.

I turned and raced to the house. There were only two routes out of Santa Amelia estates. One led to the beach road; the other to the 405 freeway. I gambled that the kidnappers were headed that way. I leaped into the seat of the Red Menace and cranked it up. In seconds, I was roaring down the drive, the car fishtailing as the limited slip differential tried to keep the immense power of its engine equally distributed to the rear wheels.

I sped past the broken gate and onto the street, heading toward the freeway. I strove in vain to spot taillights. The black sedan had a two-minute headstart. I applied more pressure on the gas pedal. I was rewarded by a forward surge of power.

I didn't catch sight of them. I covered the road to the 405 in record time. It was already seven-thirty, and luckily there was little or no traffic. When I reached the freeway entrance, I realized my mistake. The party of kidnappers wasn't headed for Los Angeles, or any entrance off the 405. They were headed toward the beach, after all. The hotel! They were going to make a clean sweep of it and wipe out Roddy's entire cadre of guards as well. That *had* to be it!

Even if I was wrong, I'd have to warn the giant García of what had happened. There was no time to retrace my route and take the beach road. There's a way to get to Newport via the freeway. It takes longer than the beach road, but I had a car that could do it quickly. Praying I wouldn't be spotted by a highway patrol car, I raced through the sparse traffic toward the Newporter Inn.

In minutes, I pulled up in front, cut the engine, and sprinted into the lobby. I headed straight for the elevators and was neatly intercepted by a house detective.

"Are you a guest here, ma'am?" he inquired.

"Friend of a guest," I said quickly. "Roddy Alcala is in trouble. I must get to him. Come with me!"

The security man hesitated, then set his heels firmly and blocked my path. "If that's true, we can find out easily enough, lady," he said. "I'll phone his suite."

"There's no time!" I protested. But I might have been talking to an inanimate object. Deliberately, the man grabbed my sore wrist and steered me to the bank of house telephones. I winced in pain.

"You'll be sorry you did this," I told him. "You don't know who you're roughing up!"

"Sure, lady," the house detective said heavily. "I apologize to your kind every time I find them and toss 'em out of here." He didn't loosen his grip on my wrist one whit. I raged inside. This rent-a-cop thought I was some groupie or fan of Roddy's, trying to get access to his room, and most likely his bed! He dialed the number for Roddy's suite.

"Ask for García," I urged. "He knows who I am."

The cop ignored me. His expression was somewhere between a sneer and a leer. It spoke volumes about what he thought of me.

"Mr. Alcala?" he said into the phone. He paused, then continued. "I have a . . . lady down here, sir. Says she knows you. . . . What's she look like? Five-four, brown hair, a little chunky . . ." The cop turned to me. "Is your name Fein, sister?"

"Doris Fein," I snapped. "And thank goodness I'm not your sister." The cop released my wrist, and I rubbed it. I'm sure he saw the indignation on my face. And I saw from his change of expression that he realized he'd made a mistake.

"Sorry, Miss Fein," he said, attempting a sickly smile. "We get all kinds of . . . oddballs here. I'm just doing my job. . . ."

"We'll see how long you're going to have that job," I said ominously as I strode toward the elevators. *Chunky,* indeed! I was so angry that it hadn't occurred to me that the house cop had spoken to Roddy. Or someone who said he was Roddy. My mind wasn't operating at one hundred percent efficiency. I'd had my wrist twisted twice tonight, and was taken for a hooker as an encore.

I rang the bell to Roddy's suite. As I pushed the button, all the things I should have thought of came crowding into my mind. I should have had Ginsberg with me. I should have called Jaime Ortega, the sheriff, to report what had happened at my home. I almost turned to go. Then the door opened and Roddy stood in the doorway. Behind him stood Pérez, one of the dark-suits I'd seen before. My curiosity was piqued and I stepped inside.

Immediately, Pérez grabbed me by the same sore wrist and hauled me into the room. Roddy made a move to come to my aid. A man I didn't recognize materialized from behind the door and savagely threw a chokehold on him. Pérez spun me toward a couch and released his grip on my wrist. I tumbled roughly to the floor and landed on a spot where I'm best able to withstand a rough landing. I looked up from the floor and surveyed the scene about me.

There were six men in the room. Roddy, Pérez, García, and three others I didn't recognize. The three strangers were aiming automatic pistols at Roddy and García. What got to me was Pérez. He wasn't being held at gunpoint like Roddy and the big man. He seemed to be in charge.

"Welcome to our little party, señorita," he said. "I must warn you, however, that it will be a quiet party. If you make any outcry, you will surely die." And to prove his point, he produced an automatic from under his dark suit coat. It had a long silencer attached to the end of the barrel!

11 / García in Action

MY MIND WAS spinning. Why was Roddy's own man, Pérez, doing this? Obviously, there was some sort of betrayal going on. I looked at Roddy. He smiled thinly and said, "It's not as confusing as it seems, Doris. Pérez is acting on orders from home."

"But from whom? I thought that he was part of your personal bodyguard."

"He is . . . was. His orders have been changed. And like a good soldier, he is following those orders."

"Has he joined the revolutionary side?"

"I told you a few times that the situation is complicated, Doris. You preferred to think I was talking down to you. No, Pérez hasn't joined the revolution. If he had, he wouldn't be aiming a pistol at me. You see, my dear, headstrong Doris, *I* am the revolution."

"Now you *have* lost me," I said.

"It began some time ago, right here in the U.S.A.,"

111

Roddy said. "In fact, in California, in San Francisco. It was there I met my sister for the first time. She was attending Berkeley."

"By sister, you're referring to Estelle Tuchman?"

Roddy raised his eyebrows. "You do know a bit about my strange family, don't you?"

"I do my best to be well informed."

"Then, as I was saying, I met Estelle. I knew she was a student there, and I knew of our relationship. I sought her out when I was able to elude my constant companions." He indicated the dark-suited men around us. "I was curious as to what sort of person she was. After all, to have a sister one has never met, this is an intriguing situation."

"And she converted you to the revolutionary side of your country's political scene?"

"Hardly. We soon discovered we had a great deal in common, besides blood. We both detested my father, the General." Roddy looked over at Pérez. "Don't worry, Pérez. Treason isn't contagious. You won't be liquidated for being in the same room with me, or hearing treason talked."

"I don't care what you speak of," Pérez responded in Spanish. "You will not have that long to talk, Major Alcala." He made the word *major* sound dirty, somehow. "We leave here in a few minutes' time." I went through the pretense of asking Roddy to explain what Pérez had said, though I'd understood. Roddy translated, then continued his story.

"You see, Doris, I never wanted to be in the military.

Perhaps I inherited my mother's artistic nature. I showed a certain talent for drawing. Then an uncle taught me some painting techniques. I learned of the world's greatest artists from him, as well. I made up my mind that I would become a painter. But one does not oppose my father's wishes in El Concepción. Not even his son may do that with impunity. For years, I went through the farce of becoming my father's heir. I endured the cruelty of the military training. And became hardened and cruel. I hated my father and I hated myself.

"I hated my own countrymen, for they were to become my responsibility; a responsibility I neither sought nor desired. In consequence, I was not a very pleasant person to be with or to know. I had no friends. That was one of the first lessons in statesmanship my father taught to me. A ruler has no friends, and anyone is a potential threat to his power."

"Uneasy is the head that wears a crown," I said.

"Not an old saying," Roddy said, nodding, "but an old truth. What sort of person would have his own brother murdered and arrange to make it look accidental? My father did that to my uncle Ramón. Poor, sweet, harmless Uncle Ramón. A gentle man, a poet. His only crime was being a homosexual and teaching his nephew, me, that there was more to the world than jackboots and bayonets."

"That's monstrous," I said, "and it doesn't even make sense. How could his teaching you about the arts be a threat to your father?"

"Don't you understand?" Roddy asked. "My father thought my contact with Uncle Ramón would contaminate me. That I, too, might become gay. As though it were contagious. Not that it mattered to him how I would live my life. It was the idea of the great General Alcala, men of men, *macho de machos,* producing such a son. It would reflect unfavorably on his own manhood."

"It sounds to me as though your father isn't too sure of *his* own manhood," I said.

"Who can say?" Roddy said, shrugging. "He has played the role of strongman for so many years, he believes he is what his propaganda says. Then, there was the way he disposed of my mother. As though she were a used handkerchief."

"He divorced her, I know."

"It was only her international fame that saved her from being murdered," Roddy said. "I found out a great deal from Estelle. My mother told the truth to Estelle's father. He respected her wishes for secrecy, even after her death. His play about her didn't tell the whole truth. It was much more bizarre.

"My mother found the General to be something less than an adequate husband and lover. It wasn't until after I was born that she discovered the brutal perversions he required to function at all. She was disgusted and repelled. She nearly went mad. Finally, a compromise was effected. In exchange for her silence, and abandoning custody of her son, the General would grant her a divorce. She never recovered from the guilt she felt at leaving me to be raised by such a monster as my father. She blamed herself for most of her short, tragic life."

"Oh my," I said. "How can you live with all this, Roddy?"

"Not very well, I'm afraid," he admitted. "I couldn't seek psychiatric help. That would be a sign of weakness in General Alcala's son. I couldn't overtly oppose my father, for son or not, I would soon be before a firing squad.

"Estelle and I devised a plan. We would have revenge upon the General in the most effective way. I would act the part of the General's heir, both morally and politically. I would also establish myself to my countrymen as a national hero, a worthy successor to the Strong Man of El Concepción.

"All this time, I would be providing to Estelle inside information about internal affairs in El Concepción. She would relay information to the revolutionary party. Locations that were unpatrolled, where arms and supplies could be landed. Sites that were relatively undefended, where guerrilla raids could be most effective. And all this time, only a handful of people inside the country knew it was I, the General's son, who masterminded the military aspect. After all, wasn't I an alumnus of your War College? I learned my lessons well, Doris."

I nodded my head toward Pérez and said, "It seems someone else knows, now."

"Obviously," Roddy agreed. "But I do not believe

these men are acting on my father's orders. My father would simply have me recalled to home and deal with me there. These men are acting on the orders of my father's 'loyal' military colleagues. I would guess Colonel Marcos and Colonel Limón. Am I correct, Pérez?"

"Does it matter, Major?" Pérez came back.

"No, I suppose not," Roddy said. "But there is something afoot at home. Something I don't know of. Otherwise these swine wouldn't dare act."

"There is indeed," I said. "I think I know what it is, too."

"You, Doris?"

"Yes, me, Doris. Your father is dying, Roddy. He made a top-secret trip to this country, to a military hospital. They confirmed what his own doctors had feared. You're about to inherit your father's throne. Evidently, the idea doesn't appeal to a number of people in your country."

"But how can you know this? How did you know about the geological survey?"

"Because she is an American intelligence agent, you idiot," snapped Pérez.

"Impossible!" Roddy came back. "She's eighteen years old. I met her completely by accident. I had her checked out. She didn't approach me. I approached her. In fact, it was difficult to even see her."

"Your father would laugh at that, *traidor*," Pérez said. "You have the soul of a mooning poet. Your naive head is filled with romance and foolish verse. You were set up by this woman and whatever agency she works for." He glanced at his watch. "But all this no longer matters. It is time to go."

"Go where?" I asked.

"Why, to Long Beach, of course," Pérez said. "You and this traitor are going for a drive. Your last on this earth."

As we took the elevator down to the lobby, Pérez spoke to us. "If you consider for even a second causing any disturbance or outcry in the lobby, think again. I am perfectly willing to kill you on the spot. If you wish to live a bit longer, I suggest you cooperate."

"If you shoot in the lobby, you're a dead man, too," I said. "You'll be seen. Stopped. There's hotel security, too."

Pérez pushed the hold button on the elevator and faced me. "You Americans are such fools," he said. "First off, your hotel security is laughable. The man isn't even armed. Second, as soon as any gunfire breaks out, witnesses scatter. Finally, if I am captured, I am prepared to die. I am a soldier. Then, too, I have diplomatic immunity from your laws."

"It doesn't cover murder of a U.S. citizen."

"An unfortunate accident, I shall say. An attempt on the life of Major Alcala . . . a successful attempt, in which you were caught in the crossfire." He removed his finger from the hold button and the car proceeded downward. "So you will cooperate, won't you?"

It was a convincing argument. Especially with the silencer-tipped pistol nudging me from behind. The lobby was deserted anyway. I didn't even see the rent-a-cop who had detained me earlier. Roddy, García, and I were shoved into the Mercedes sedan, covered by Pérez and his pistol. One of the dark-suits drove it, while the other two took my keys and drove the Red Menace behind us.

In a half-hour we were in Long Beach, entering the track area. Track security recognized our little party and waved us through. Despite the late hour, many of the pits were lighted up, and last-minute work was being done on the cars that would race the next day. We stopped at the El Concepción team's assigned area and were roughly hustled out of the Mercedes. We were forced to sit on the greasy ground, our backs resting against the wall of the pit. I looked at Roddy, and at the giant, García. Their faces were totally impassive.

Pérez spoke rapidly to one of the dark-suits, who went into the trunk of the Mercedes sedan and came out with a set of coveralls, which he quickly donned. He then opened a standing tool chest in the pit. To my great distress, he got into my beautiful red car and pulled it up alongside the tool chest.

"Your car is a marvelous piece of machinery, señorita," Pérez said. "So marvelous that Major Alcala is going to drive you both around the track." He reached inside his coat and produced a bottle of whiskey. "Unfortunately, you have both been drinking a bit. A dangerous thing to do when handling a high-performance car. You will have an accident which neither of you will survive. Your steering mechanism will fail, and with a full gas tank . . ."

"And what makes you think we'll just drive off?"

"Oh, we don't need your cooperation, señorita. Both you and the Major will be belted into your seats. The throttle will be preset to full race by my mechanic. He is about to do that now. You and the Major will already be unconscious."

Pérez handed his pistol to one of the dark-suits and approached me, bottle of whiskey in hand. "And now it's time you had a little drink, señorita," he said. He grabbed my hair and tilted the opened bottle toward my mouth, spilling a good amount all over my driving suit. I smelled the reek of the whiskey and I pressed my lips together tight. To no avail. He simply held my nose until I had to open my mouth.

A few feet away, the mechanic working on my car cranked up the engine at full throttle. It made a roar that would have stopped traffic anyplace else. But with engines turning over all about us, it went unnoticed. The mechanic then got one of those creepers, a low platform on wheels that would allow him to lie on his back and slide under the car to sabotage the steering.

Satisfied that I'd swallowed enough whiskey to show up on an autopsy report, Pérez moved toward Roddy with the bottle. To do so, he had to pass quite close to the giant, García. Suddenly, the huge man sprang to his feet like a great cat. He lunged at Pérez and grabbed him by the throat, simultaneously spinning him around. Pérez was now between García and his own gunman.

The dark-suit fired his pistol just the same. Pérez was an inadequate shield for so large a man as García. I saw the big man's frame jolted by the impact of the shot.

Roddy, meantime, was already on his feet and had become a whirling dervish of destruction on the nearby dark-suits. His karate training wasn't just some words on a dossier. One of the dark-suits was already on the ground, writhing in agony.

I saw my chance, and I took it. Grabbing a wrench from the tool chest, I ran to the Red Menace and hammered as hard a shot as I could on the shins of the mechanic's legs, protruding from under the car. I then vaulted into the driver's seat of my car.

"Roddy! Over here!" I cried. The engine was still at full throttle, and no amount of my working the gas pedal had any effect. Roddy chopped at the remaining dark-suit and sprinted the few feet to where I sat in the car. The fallen man produced a revolver and fired, just before Roddy leaped into the seat alongside me.

Roddy faltered, then got the rest of the way into my car. He'd been hit! A bullet starred the windshield inches away from my face. I jammed the car into gear and popped the clutch. With a scream of tortured rubber, the Red Menace took off like an antelope goosed by a cattle prod. One of the dark-suits caromed off the right front fender as I guided the sluing car out of the pits and onto the track.

The remaining dark-suits fired at us and then began getting into the Mercedes sedan. Desperately trying to control the car, I roared down the straightaway toward the first turn.

"Can you handle the car?" Roddy asked, his face distorted with pain as he clutched at his shoulder.

"Depends on whether that guy had time to wreck the steering," I shouted over the roar of the engine. "We'll know soon enough. Here comes the first turn!"

12/ A Wild Ride

WE THUNDERED INTO the turn too fast for safety. I tried
to remember all my lessons from Jimmy Ogilvie. Brake,
find the "groove" of the turn. Make the turn and accelerate coming out. It worked like a charm. The black
sedan was wallowing through the difficult turn and
receding rapidly in my rear-view mirror.

The engine of my car was roaring in protest. But I
had to stay in first gear. If I upshifted, the full race
throttle would send us hurtling down the track even
faster. As it was, the car would do over a hundred miles
per hour in first gear. I could have cut off the ignition,
but then the sedan would overtake us. Talk about your
Catch-22!

I knew I had to draw attention to our plight, but how?
To blow the horn or flash the lights meant nothing. The
horn wouldn't be heard, and no one was on the course

to notice me flashing. We were coming down the first straightaway when I saw the escape road at the far end, at the second turn.

Because the race is run over city streets, and permanent crash barriers can't be put up, there are small cutoffs at the curves, in case a car is traveling too fast to negotiate the turn. In this case, the cutoff led to another city street, cleared for the purpose. I headed for the cutoff and braked as best I was able. The sedan had begun to close the gap. Shortly, unless I could do something—anything—the pursuers would be in pistol range. I swung out onto regular city streets. Oh, for a police car! But there was nothing. The late hour found downtown Long Beach absolutely deserted.

I saw a trailblazer sign for the 405 freeway. By slipping the clutch and braking, I negotiated the turn. In a few hair-raising minutes I was on the freeway. Still no traffic, still no sign of a Highway Patrol car. And still the relentless Mercedes behind us. I shifted into second gear, and the Red Menace responded with a surge forward. Despite the fact that we were traveling at seventy-five miles per hour, the tires chirped on the pavement to the upshift. The speedometer climbed over the century mark.

I nearly cried with relief when we flashed by an overpass and I saw a black-and-white patrol car entering. He'd seen us and was giving pursuit! But just as the patrol car was gaining access to the freeway, the Mercedes came thundering by. The patrol car caught a glancing blow, and I saw it go off the road. The Mercedes staggered like a fighter after a stiff punch has rocked him, but continued after us.

The exits flashed by so quickly at these speeds that they seemed only seconds apart. We sped past the exit for L.A. International Airport. As ever, there was traffic near LAX, but at this hour, it was light. Then I recalled the exits still to go. If I could put enough distance between us and the pursuing car, I could negotiate the off ramp for Westwood by slowing down.

My plan was a simple one. Just a few blocks from the Westwood off ramp is the Federal Building, the very location where the picture of Estelle Tuchman had been taken. They have a positively huge parking lot there. They also have the office of the Federal Bureau of Investigation, and, I knew, the West Coast headquarters of the IGO. Somebody would be bound to notice a car roaring around.

"Hang on, Roddy," I cried over the engine noise. "We're getting off the freeway. I hope!"

"I'm with you," he said weakly.

Although it was dangerous, I took my eyes off the road to glance at him. He was slumped down in the passenger seat and *verry* pale. He'd been losing blood from the shoulder wound.

Tires squealed as I braked and slipped the clutch enough to make my turnoff. I didn't know if the black car was still behind me. I was too busy staying alive to check. We racketed down the winding off ramp and I nearly lost control on the curve. Inanely, I giggled as we flashed past the yellow sign that read EXIT SPEED: 35 MPH. The Red Menace is a superbly designed car. We took the curve at better than twice that speed. Still it held the road.

I thought of my plan and hoped desperately we'd be seen on the streets of Westwood. In a flash we were at the parking lot entrance to the Federal Building. Briefly, we were airborne as we tore up the incline from the curb. Then all four wheels made contact with pavement and away we went again.

The Red Menace has a turning circle of forty feet. I began looping around in the empty parking lot at a ridiculous rate of speed. It was not unlike being on one of those amusement park rides. Except that if I lost concentration for even a few seconds, we'd be rolling over and over. Or worse, end for end.

Fortunately, the car's controls are well laid out. I was able to reach the horn control without relinquishing my two-handed grip on the wheel. And the Klaxon is loud. I was making my third turn when the Mercedes, somewhat battered from its brush with the patrol car, entered the parking lot.

Were these men insane? If they tried to carry out their plan to kill us, there was no way they could cover it up. They had been seen by the police. But as Pérez had pointed out, he was prepared to die himself to carry out his orders. The black car headed toward us and a window slid down. I saw the face of one of the dark-suits and, worse, I saw the business end of a pistol.

I yanked hard on the wheel and sped at the black car head on, presenting less of a target. Now, if the prospect of a car at high speed coming straight at him didn't spook the driver of the black car, I was in deep trouble. But I was counting on the driver not knowing some California folk customs.

The game is called "Chicken," and it has taken its toll of young drivers in Southern California over the years. Two cars head straight for each other at high speed. The first driver to turn away to avoid sudden, crunching death is Chicken. Horrendous as it sounds, and is, the "game" is still played here. By people with no sense at all, I might add.

Luck was with me. The driver didn't know the custom. He turned away well before we were anywhere near him. I zipped past the black car, did a 180, and headed back toward him again. I saw the dark-suit lean out of the window and aim at us as I made the next Chicken run. Involuntarily, I crouched low behind the wheel, simultaneously screaming at Roddy, "Get down!"

This time the other driver held fast, and bullets sang by as the space between us closed. I thought for a moment that the driver *was* prepared to die. At the last second, I pulled aside. We passed so close that we brushed against the side of the Mercedes. We also nicked the gunman hanging out of the window. I heard a scream of pain as we passed. As I swung the car around again, I saw that his arm had been hit. The pistol lay on the pavement of the parking lot.

Then, suddenly, it seemed the world was filled with flashing lights and sirens. Black-and-white Highway Patrol cars began streaming into the lot. A piercing light shone down on us from above, and the thunderous *chop-chop* of helicopter rotors drowned out the noise around us. A voice from over a bullhorn on the helicopter roared down at us, "This is the police. Stop your vehicles and come out with your hands up!"

I suppose Pérez and his henchmen knew the game was up. But that didn't stop them from making one last try. The car came to a halt, and Pérez tumbled out, hit the ground rolling, and came up firing at us.

He hadn't emptied his automatic when answering fire came from all directions. He staggered from the impact of shots from three directions and fell to the pavement. The other men came out of the car with their hands in the air.

With a sigh of relief, I cut the ignition and brought the Red Menace to a halt. Police swarmed onto the scene, and one of them, pistol drawn, raced up to the passenger side of the car.

"Out, both of you," he commanded. He assumed the two-handed grip and aiming stance I'd seen so often in films.

"That man is wounded," I said as I got out. "He can't move."

"Stand clear of the vehicle, lady," the cop replied, and came closer to inspect the now unconscious Roddy.

"I'm an employee of the U.S. government," I told the

cop. "The wounded man is a member of a foreign government."

"Yeah, and I'm the Queen of England," the policeman responded. "You just do as you're ordered."

I did. In short order, I was spread across the hood of my car and handcuffed. I was put into the back of a patrol car, and just as the car left to take me to the Westwood police station, an ambulance arrived, and I saw the white-clad men attending to Roddy. It was about then that the reaction to my wild ride and several brushes with death per minute set in. I began to shake uncontrollably, and though it embarrassed me terribly, I also began to cry. I cried all the way to jail and into the detention cell they put me in.

I don't know how much later it was that Speedy Ginsberg came to get me out of my cell. I was seated on the hard, unpadded bench when he arrived with a uniformed policeman, who unlocked the door.

"Well, good morning, Doris," he said cheerily.

"Are you sure they call you Speedy?" I said without preamble. "I've been here forever. What time is it? They took my watch."

"Eight-fifteen A.M.," Ginsberg said. "I've only known you were here since seven-thirty. That's prompt enough, isn't it?"

"And where were you while I was trying to stay alive?" I went on. "Do you know what's been going on?"

"Whoa . . . whoa!" Ginsberg said, holding up a hand. "First off, keeping guard on Roddy isn't IGO turf. It's FBI, and only if they think it necessary. Be mad at them, not me. The one agent we had was gathering information, that's all."

"Then where was that one agent?"

"Have you forgotten? *You* were the one agent we had on the scene. I was doing paper work most of the night. So far as I knew, all was well. I hadn't heard from you and assumed you were home in bed. I turned in about two and got the call from the police at seven-thirty. And here I am."

"Then get me out of here," I begged. "I have to have a bath and some sleep before I go bonkers."

"Not that easy, Doris. I have to post bail and confer with our lawyers. And I need a full report from you to send to Maryland immediately."

"Where's Roddy Alcala, and how is he?" I asked.

"In a private, guarded room in a private hospital in Beverly Hills. He'll be fine."

"Then get your information from Roddy," I said. "I'm too bushed to even talk straight." Then, what Ginsberg said sank in on me. "Bail? What for? I didn't do anything criminal!"

"Not in the larger sense, no," Ginsberg said. "But so far as the Highway Patrol and several local police agencies are concerned, you're a menace and a public danger. You've broken almost every motor vehicle ordinance on the books and fled to avoid arrest. . . ."

"But that was in the line of duty," I protested. "I was on government business."

"On *secret* government business," Ginsberg added. "We don't want this in the papers, now, do we?"

"If you don't want it on the front page of *my* newspaper, you get this cleared up," I said.

"Doris, Doris," Speedy chided, "you must really read what you sign. Your contract with the company is quite clear about leaking secret data to the press. There are some serious penalties and disciplinary actions for that."

"All right, all right," I said resignedly, "just get me out of here. Is there anything that says you can't take my report at my home?"

"No, that'll be fine. I'll drive you, once we get the paper work cleared up here."

"My car is still drivable, isn't it? I know it's had the throttle jammed. But that's a simple snap adjustment."

"That may be so, Doris," Ginsberg said, "but your car is impounded. And so is your license to drive until the charges are resolved."

"Oh no," I moaned. "If this is how the IGO rewards their employees for a job well done . . ."

"The reward of good work is the knowledge that you've done it," Ginsberg said.

"Is that a quote?"

"You betcha," Speedy said grinning. "George T. Case said it to me years ago. And he repeats it every time I want a vacation or a salary review."

"It sounds like him," I admitted. I followed Ginsberg and the turnkey down the hall to where freedom supposedly waited. I made up my mind that I was going to have a long chat with George Case. Not a fireside chat, either. Unless he was turning on a spit.

13/ Dr. Cane and Mr. Alcala

"MORE DESSERT, DR. CANE?" I asked. "Bruno made it especially for my guests. I don't eat desserts." I heard a low growl from Petunia. I think she said *Liar!*

"I'd explode if I ate another mouthful," the young veterinarian answered.

"I have no such qualms, m'dear," drawled Vick Knight. "I'll have another helping, Bruno."

"You also have a shorter fuse," quipped his wife. "I may stand clear."

"I'll have no remarks about my fuse," he W.C.'d.

"Much ado about nothing?" I inquired.

"Surrounded by assassins," Vick grumbled. "And speaking of such things, whatever happened with your Caribbean friend—what was his name?"

"Alcala," I replied, "and don't kid me, Vick Knight. You never forget a name or address. That's why, when you got married, you raffled off your little black

131

book. It was an empty gesture."

"It was bought by the Rams' offensive line," Vick said. "And even so, they still couldn't score."

"If you're really curious about Roddy Alcala," I said, "all you have to do is pick up today's *Register.*"

"I missed the paper today. We're busy with the benefit performance of the circus."

"A big to-do," I said. "He's announced that free elections will be held in El Concepción this fall."

"About time, too," Vick said. "He's turned out to be a big surprise, that lad. His father's regime was the most repressive in recent memory, and his new government promises to be quite progressive. For a Central American state, that is."

"Well, I'll believe it when I see it," I said. "I spent a lot of time with Roddy. He has a lot of nineteenth-century ideas."

"Doesn't make him a bad guy," Vick said. "We've had a few progressive nineteenth-century presidents in this country. In fact, the one we've got."

"Please, no more politics, Vick," Carolyn said. "Bad for digestion."

"You're right. There's a lot of stuff going on in Washington I can't stomach," he replied.

"Well, I can't swallow another bite," Dr. Cane said. "And I have an early day tomorrow. Have to see some horse people."

"That's what I like," Vick said, "a doctor who makes horse calls."

"Not funny," I said, deadpan.

"At least I didn't make a reference to horsepower. Not to mention your car."

"What about my car?"

"I told you not to mention it. But you're taking me too seriously." He smiled. "Which is more than my wife does. I just wanted to know how it's going. And when I get to drive it."

"*I* only get to drive it starting this coming week. That's when my suspension is over. Just as well, though. I had to replace the windshield."

"A thrown stone?"

"No, several fired bullets. I was in the middle when some people decided to do away with Roddy Alcala. Going out with a Caribbean politico can be dangerous, it seems."

"This is fascinating," Carolyn said. "I didn't see a thing on TV or in the papers about it."

"You weren't supposed to," I said. "It was all hush-hush. I tried to get away from the fireworks as fast as I could," I added, half-truthfully. "In the process, I collected a speeding ticket and a sixty-day suspension of my driver's license."

"Well, it *is* a fast car," Vick said.

"It must be," Dr. Cane said, "to get you a suspension that long."

"It's all over, and not very good as a topic for conversation," I said.

Tactfully, Dr. Cane took the hint. He stood up and said, "Well, I have to be speeding off, myself. My horse calls, you know."

"Ouch," said Vick. "It isn't near as funny when somebody else says it."

I walked Dr. Cane to the door while Vick and Carolyn finished their desserts. Outside, the Rovers came rushing up to greet us both. Rover One, the dog who'd been hit by the motorcycle a few months ago, was most effusive toward Cane.

"I've been meaning to ask you," I said to him, "about the time Rover got hurt. You knew immediately he'd had a run-in with a motorcycle. Yet I didn't tell you, and certainly Bruno didn't."

"He isn't very chatty, is he?" Cane agreed.

"And that isn't an answer," I said firmly. "How did you know what caused Rover's injuries?"

"The injury was caused by a single wheel rolling over his body. A car would have hit him and thrown him."

"A car at slow speed could have rolled over him with one wheel."

"Yes, but the greater weight of a car would have caused much more damage. He'd have died." Cane paused and a sly look came over his face. "Of course, there's one other explanation. . . ."

"Namely?"

"Rover told me, himself."

"Great Scott!" I cried. "Can this be the famous Dr. Doolittle I've been dining with? Complete with a chorus of 'Talk to the Animals'?"

"They say a good vet can understand what animals say. Who knows?" He got into his Volkswagen van and started up the engine.

"Be careful of the Rovers driving out," I admonished.

"Not to worry," Cane said with a huge wink. "I told them to stay clear."

I watched him drive away, and saw that Bruno had buzzed the gate release to let him out. Then I went back into the house. I found Vick and Carolyn just ready to go.

"So soon?" I asked.

"The dawn comes up like thunder, and there's that benefit for CHOC coming up," Vick explained. "Your mom's on the committee, Doris. I'll say hello to her for you at the meeting tomorrow."

"Conspiracy," I pronounced. "I haven't called her in two days. Has she been after you to call me, to call her?"

"I'll never tell," Vick said with a puckish smile. "But just in case, call your mama, huh?"

"All right, all right. Sheesh, what a *nudzh!*"

Good-byes took as long as they usually do with Vick. He can't bear to leave without a funny exit line. After they'd gone, I went to my study to review the crime reports in the papers. I knew Bruno would be up to enter the stories in the computer after he had cleared away the dinner things. As he's so much faster on the computer keyboard than I, he actually encodes the entries.

Because I had some time, I thought of calling Helen Grayson. She was on Santa Catarina Island for the day. She'd been renting her cottage there, and some trouble with the plumbing had developed. And there was no doubt I had to call my mother. She'd been trying to pry the truth out of me about the Alcala case, and I'd just as determinedly been avoiding the topic. Well, no sense in putting things off. I reached for the phone and was startled when it rang just as I touched it.

"I have a person-to-person call for Ms. Doris Fein," the operator said.

"This is she. Go ahead."

"Hello, Doris? This is Roddy Alcala."

"Speak of the devil, or whatever your role is this week. How are you, Roddy? How's the shoulder?"

"Almost completely healed. I still can't return salutes too well. And that doesn't anger me, either. But after this fall, I won't have to."

"You're really going to step down?"

"Better than that. I'm going to France to study painting after the elections are over."

"Congratulations, Roddy. Tell me, why the phone call? I haven't seen you or spoken a word with you in two months. Have you decided silence isn't golden after all?"

"Forgive me, Doris. You must understand that when I got home, the country was in chaos. My father dead by an assassin's bullet, the conspiracy of the colonels . . . Ironic, though. All they had to do was wait a few months. My father would have died without a gunshot."

"I still don't know what happened there in El Concepción," I said. "Evidently, your governmental reforms don't extend to freedom of the press. There's been a blackout on all but the most innocuous of items coming out of your country."

"A temporary measure. Things will be better very shortly. The provisional government is coming along. In fact, all I'm doing now is waiting for fall and the elections to bow out completely." He paused. "Uh, Doris . . ."

"Yes, Roddy?"

"I could really explain all this much better in person."

"In person? Where are you calling from?"

"Washington, D.C. I've just completed a leasing deal with some oil companies and your government. I could fly directly home, or I could make a stopoff in California. If I'm welcome, that is."

"Frankly, I don't know," I said. "It tends to be dangerous hanging around with you, señor."

"All in the past, Doris. Say you'll see me. Please?"

"The magic word to a woman, when spoken by a macho," I replied. "Okay, I'll see you. When and where?"

"I'm flying military. I can get a courtesy landing at El Toro Marine Air Base. I can be there in four hours."

"Four hours? It's already ten-thirty at night here. And what kind of plane can get here in four hours?"

"I told you it was a military jet. And I'm flying it myself."

"Tell you what, Roddy," I suggested. "You get some sleep and we'll make it lunch at La Strada."

"Very sentimental and romantic," he said. "It's where we first met for dinner. It seems ages ago."

"Time flies when you're having fun, eh? Good night, Roddy."

"Good night, Doris. *Hasta la vista.* Until I see you again."

It was sinful of me, but I had the Veal Scallopini Francese. Sautéed veal scallops with lemon. Petunia was overjoyed and kept pressing for pasta to go with it. I prevailed, though. I had a simple hearts of celery vinaigrette. Roddy had a seafood crepe and a salad.

He sighed expansively after the last mouthful and sat back in his chair. We'd chatted lightly over lunch. No serious topics, and definitely nothing political. I could see he was getting set to make a pronouncement of some sort.

"Pues bien, dígame," I said, meaning: Very well, tell me. A look of astonishment came over Roddy's face.

"¿Porqué no me dijiste que tu hablas español?" he asked, meaning: Why didn't you tell me you spoke Spanish?

"You never asked me," I replied in Spanish. "And I don't speak that well. I'm more comfortable in English, or French. But you knew I spoke French, didn't you? You called to me that night of the wild drive to warn García. And how is García? I have a million questions."

"García is well and healthy. His wound was superficial, but enough to render him unconscious. He is a bull of a man. It would take more than a scalp shot to harm him."

"Are you telling me he was shot in the head, and he's fine?"

"As I say, a bull of a man. And most loyal. You know, he is only five years older than I? In my childhood, he was both my playmate and my protector. He continues his role, even today."

"I don't see him," I said joking, and looking around the dining room.

"He is back at El Toro. Happily, I don't need body-guards any longer."

"It all seems to have worked out for you, Roddy," I said. "Your father never did find out you were working against him. You inherited the power with no armed uprising. Or so I would guess."

"There was quite a bit of gunplay, but only when the colonels were arrested. Being what they were, one de-cided to shoot it out with the soldiers who came for him. Colonel Limón, however, directed only one shot: at his left temple."

"Falling on his sword being out of fashion?"

"You might say so. It all goes with this . . ." He in-dicated his garb. He was wearing the uniform of an air force major in the El Concepción army. He did look impressive and quite handsome, in a military way. When I first saw him, I'd asked why the uniform. He'd explained that because his transportation and landing place were extensions of military courtesy by our gov-ernment, he had to remain in uniform.

"But soon I'll be out of this monkey suit forever," he said. "I shall be able to lead a life of my own. The one I wanted to begin with."

"And no more fast cars?" I asked.

"That was to gain the respect of my people. It worked, too. Even though I never brought home the Great Fish, what I had done was enough. I am disbanding the racing team. It has served its purpose."

"The leopard's spots are changing?" I asked with raised eyebrows.

"Not entirely. For instance, I will be ordering a Cavalieri automobile on my next trip to California, in the fall."

"You're not going directly to Paris?"

"No. I shall be visiting my sister, in San Francisco. She has taken a place near there, in Marin County. And when I do return, I would like to see more of you, Doris."

"Don't remind me of what I had for lunch. A few more La Strada lunches and you'll be seeing *much* more of me."

"I don't know why you speak so," Roddy said, leaning across the table and taking my hand. "I was attracted to you immediately. You were intelligent, drove well, had a quick wit. So like the woman I most admired in this country."

"Oh really?' " I said coolly. "Who might she be?"

"My sister, Estelle."

I burst into raucous laughter. "Oh, Roddy," I said after I'd wiped my eyes with a napkin. "I don't know whether to be insulted or flattered. You were attracted to me because I reminded you of your sister?"

"In my country, that is a compliment. A man honors his sister as he would his mother," he said somewhat stiffly. I saw he was quite serious.

"I'm sorry, Roddy," I said. "I meant no offense. But you *do* know that 'you remind me of my sister' is one of the oldest come-on lines in the world, don't you? At least in California it is."

"That is not how I meant it."

"I know that. Now. But you were saying about how devilishly attractive I am?"

"It's true. I even forgave you lying to me about being an IGO agent."

"You knew all along?"

"No. I suspected you were in someone's employ, but I didn't know whose. I later found out from your Mr. Case . . ."

"He is definitely not *my* Mr. Case," I put in.

"Strange. He spoke well of you, Doris. He said that if you had the proper attitude, you would be a good operative. He also respected your stand about secret police agencies, and understood why you will not be an agent on a regular basis."

"This from George Case? I can hardly believe my ears."

"You disbelieve my feelings for you, as well. And you have not answered my question. Will we be able to see each other in the fall?"

I looked across the table at Roderigo Alfonso Alcala.

He was a *verry* handsome man. He was intelligent, brave, and, when he chose to be, extremely charming. But I wondered about that charm. I'd seen it slip away like a veneer when he'd grabbed my wrist that night.

And through our entire conversation, there had been no mention of one salient fact. I had saved Roddy's life. Scared green, and not at all sure of what I had been doing, the fact was indisputable. I had saved this charming fellow's life. And not got so much as a thank-you. Maybe the silly code under which he'd been raised made him less a man for thanking me. I don't know. I felt the gratitude. I knew it was there, but Roddy hadn't actually come out and thanked me. Or maybe I was the ego-tripper here, demanding my due. What had Case said about not thanking a professional for merely doing her job?

There was a lot to be said for Roddy. But I suspected that once on his home ground, the typical macho attitudes would come to the fore. Leopards don't change their spots; they can't. Despite his artistic leanings and liberal attitudes, Roddy was still the General's son. He'd been raised in a tradition that is antithetical to all I stand for in both human and women's rights.

I gave his hand a little squeeze and said, "Call me in the fall. After the free elections. We'll talk then, Roddy."